"So, a man who coo

some lucky lady snapped you up?"

"There's been no one recently I've wanted to be involved with."

"Oh, I'm sorry." *Sort of.*

A swarm of butterflies swooped in Lindsay's stomach.

"I was a lonely kid," he said. "The kind of lonely that can only be understood by someone who's felt it, too. You know, not belonging. I can't imagine that you were that kind of kid."

"Ah, but I was," she said. "Sometimes I still am."

"I don't believe it." His voice was a sexy whisper.

Then he kissed her. His mouth was so inviting, and even though a voice of reason sounded in a distant fog in the back of her mind—she really shouldn't be doing this—she had to have one more taste.

Dear Reader,

I have a confession to make: even though I'm not a terrific cook, I eat up the Food Network and cooking shows on other channels, such as *Top Chef.* I can't get enough of them. From BBQ to beautifully baked cakes (and everything in between), I devour these tasty shows.

On the upside, this indulgence has greatly improved my previously limited culinary repertoire. It also started the wheels turning for *Accidental Cinderella.* I've always wondered about the stories behind these shows; how did these Food Network stars make the leap from the kitchen to cable? That question inspired this book. In these pages I explore what happens when you take an unlikely cooking/travel show host and mix her up with a bad-boy chef in desperate need of redemption. The result is deliciously sweet and spicy.

I hope you'll have as much fun reading *Accidental Cinderella* as I had writing it!

Bon appétit!

Nancy Robards Thompson

ACCIDENTAL CINDERELLA

NANCY ROBARDS THOMPSON

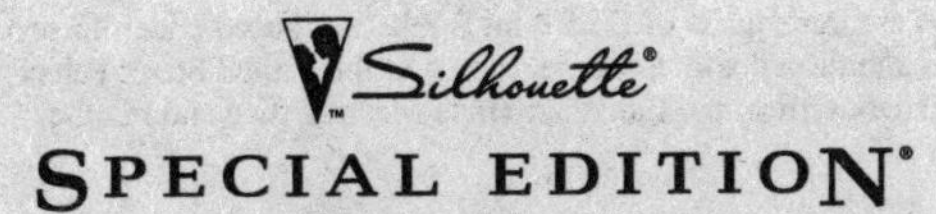

Published by Silhouette Books
America's Publisher of Contemporary Romance

Recycling programs for this product may not exist in your area.

ISBN-13: 978-0-373-65484-0

ACCIDENTAL CINDERELLA

This edition published by arrangement with Harlequin Books S.A.

Visit Silhouette Books at www.eHarlequin.com

Printed in U.S.A.

Books by Nancy Robards Thompson

Silhouette Special Edition

Accidental Princess #1931
Accidental Cinderella #2002

Harlequin NEXT

Out with the Old, In with the New
What Happens in Paris (Stays in Paris?)
Sisters
True Confessions of the Stratford Park PTA
Like Mother, Like Daughter (But in a Good Way)
"Becoming My Mother..."
Beauty Shop Tales
An Angel in Provence

NANCY ROBARDS THOMPSON

Award-winning author Nancy Robards Thompson is a sister, wife and mother who has lived the majority of her life south of the Mason-Dixon line. As the oldest sibling, she reveled in her ability to make her brother laugh at inappropriate moments and she soon learned she could get away with it by proclaiming, "What? I wasn't doing anything." It's no wonder that upon graduating from college with a degree in journalism, she discovered that reporting "just the facts" bored her silly. Since hanging up her press pass to write novels full-time, critics have deemed her books "funny, smart and observant." She loves chocolate, champagne, cats and art (though not necessarily in that order). When she's not writing, she enjoys spending time with her family, reading, hiking and doing yoga.

For Michael, for all the wonderful meals over the years.

Chapter One

"You almost make a girl believe in fairy tales." In this rare intimate moment amidst the festive chaos, Lindsay Bingham reached out and tucked a stray strand of hair into her friend Sophie Baldwin's bridal veil.

Sophie looked every bit the princess she was. Literally. *A real princess.*

The wedding was magical and the reception was the social ticket of the year, Lindsay marveled. It was still hard to believe that salt-of-the-earth Sophie Baldwin from Trevard, North Carolina, was full-fledged royalty.

Last year, she'd discovered her birthright—or maybe it was more apropos to say her birthright finally found her—and she'd been swept away to the island of St. Michel in imperial fashion. As if that weren't enough good fortune, she'd just married her prince in a gorgeous December wedding.

Right on cue, tall, handsome Luc Lejardin whirled by on the dance floor with another woman in his arms. But as he caught and held his bride's gaze, it was perfectly clear he only had eyes for one woman.

Lindsay sighed. She would've gladly relinquished rights to an entire kingdom to have a man look at her that way.

"If I keep humming, 'Wish Upon A Star,' will I get my turn as Cinderella?"

Sophie smiled. "Maybe, but since that song belongs to Pinocchio, you might end up with a fibbing bad boy rather than a handsome prince."

Fibbing bad boys. The story of her life.

"That's right," she conceded. "Cinderella's fight song was 'A Dream Is a Wish Your Heart Makes....'"

Sophie winked at her. "A little dream-wishing never hurt anyone."

"Yeah, but for the foreseeable future, I'm going to do my best to do more than dream. I'm getting my life together. I'm calling it the 'New Me' plan."

Yeah, rather than the old "Plan of Self-Destruction." A strategy that involved seeing how many years she could accrue at her dead-end job as a receptionist at Trevard Social Services and how many Mr. Wrongs she could pack into one lifetime.

She sighed against the beat of protest that thrummed inside her. Frankly, her "New Me" plan was a lot easier in theory than in practice. Her receptionist job was comfortable. It was so simple she could do it on autopilot. Even though her boss was a colossal pain in the butt, it was definitely one of those *devil-you-know* situations. Or so she told herself.

But the job was getting her nowhere.

As were the men she sometimes dated.

From her perspective, the journey toward true love sometimes seemed akin to walking a tightrope strung across a dark, scary abyss. She'd walked that rope before, holding the hand of a man she loved and trusted, a man who, once upon a time, said he wanted to spend the rest of his life with her. Ultimately, he'd not just let go of her hand; he'd shoved her into the darkness below.

She'd nearly drowned in the misery.

Even now, almost seven years later, when she thought about the man who'd broken her heart, the pain resurfaced like it was covered by fading Novocain.

To numb herself, she dated. She'd even had relationships—if you could call them that. The men all had one thing in common beyond the tall, broad-shouldered, feral masculinity: none were husband material.

She preferred it that way. By dating the perennial bad boy, it was a given that those relationships wouldn't last. She kept a firm grip on her heart. That way it couldn't be broken.

Sophie squeezed Lindsay's hand. "I think focusing on *you* is a wonderful idea, and to help you with that, I have a surprise for you." Sophie's face lit with a certain look Lindsay had seen before. A look that meant Lindsay should probably run the other way—as fast as she could.

Her friend always meant well, and she could also be extraordinarily generous, as evidenced by the way she'd packed the past month full of fabulous surprises—from daylong, head-to-toe spa days, to designer clothes, shoes and handbags, to the custom-made Cartier diamond necklace and earrings she'd presented her attendants to wear with their bridesmaids dresses.

"What are you up to now?" Lindsay narrowed her eyes, playing along with the tone Sophie had set for this one.

"I'll tell you in a minute. First, I have to say hello to someone."

She followed Sophie's gaze to a short, slight man who was making his way toward them.

"Your highness, such a lovely wedding." The man had a thick Italian accent. He bowed and dusted Sophie's hand with a kiss. "It is a great honor to bear witness to such a momentous occasion."

Okay, this could take a while. But Lindsay had monopolized Sophie long enough. It was time to relinquish her friend and give others a turn. It was a good time to get a drink. The guests didn't want to talk to her, and that was okay. Really, it was. She didn't want to stand there, awkward as a sixth finger while this man did what every guest at this wedding endeavored to do: endear himself to the future queen of St. Michel.

She turned to Sophie. "Will you excuse me for a moment?"

Sophie smiled. "Is everything okay?"

Lindsay nodded. "Absolutely, I need something to drink. Would either of you care for something?"

"Nothing for me," said the Italian. "But please allow me to be at your service."

"No, no, thank you. You stay here and talk. I'll be back."

"You don't have to leave," Sophie whispered.

She'd been so good to make sure Lindsay didn't feel out of place during her stay at the palace. The poor woman must be exhausted.

"I'm fine," Lindsay assured her. "I'll find you later."

"Okay, don't forget. Your surprise."

Sophie had been so generous already. Lindsay couldn't imagine what else she could pull out of her crown. Especially tonight. Sophie's big night. It felt wrong for her friend to take time away from her wedding to give her something else. If anyone should be fussed over tonight, it was the bride.

Across the room, Lindsay spied a tux-clad server with a tray of champagne flutes. She walked over and helped herself, then turned to survey the crowd. The guest list was studded with several A-listers who melded so well with the others that sometimes Lindsay had to do a double take before she could identify them. But she was careful to not be too obvious. No one here gawked or gushed.

That's why it was important that she honored the agreement she'd made with herself and remained cool—and not go stark raving fan girl, even though *Johnny Depp* was sitting directly in her line of vision at a table for two, with his arm draped around a petite woman.

Lindsay bit her bottom lip instead.

Johnny. Depp.

She watched as the actor lifted a cigarette to his lips, taking a long drag. It was just as well she didn't try to engage him in conversation, because with all this pent-up nervous energy, she'd probably end up saying the wrong thing or bleating like a startled goat rather than forming words that made any sense.

Her toes curled in her custom-made Jimmy Choos (one of the bridesmaid gifts from Sophie), and she exhaled a full-body sigh, reluctantly tearing her gaze from him.

As she skimmed the crowd, she stopped suddenly, backtracking to a familiar face. A sulking hulk of handsomeness and broad shoulders sat alone at a table toward the back of the ballroom.

It was that famous chef. Oh, what was his name…?

As she studied his ruggedly attractive face, the olive skin and perpetual five o'clock shadow, Lindsay's mind flipped through names one by one, but she couldn't quite pin it down.

A couple of years ago, he'd been the poster boy of the trashy tabloids. Oh, what was his name…? He used to have a show on Food TV…but something had happened. She couldn't remember what. In fact, she couldn't remember the last time she'd seen him on television. Not that she'd ever been a big fan—but boy, he was even better-looking in person than on TV, and the tabloid photos didn't do him justice.

Montigo.

Carlos Montigo.

Yes! That was it.

She snapped her fingers. As if he'd heard her, which was impossible over the clamor of conversation and music, his dark gaze slid to hers and locked into place.

Her stomach performed a curious lurching summersault. Good grief, the guy was handsome. But based on the headlines, he was no Prince Charming. Not by any stretch of the imagination.

Still, she couldn't make herself look away.

Ping. There it was. That steel-to-bad boy magnetic draw of attraction—pulling her in a direction her better judgment warned she shouldn't go.

He kept watching her and she kept watching him back, over the top of her champagne flute.

She'd known guys with bad reputations like him. He was exactly the type of guy she was drawn to.

If there was one thing her résumé of postengagement relationships had taught her it was you can't rehabilitate a bad boy.

That was the short-term draw.

A slow, lopsided smile that barely turned up the corner of Montigo's lips promised trouble. Those were definitely bad-boy eyes gazing at her. Dark, sexy, bad-boy eyes that were meandering brazenly down the length of her body.

It wasn't the way Luc looked at Sophie. No, this was something altogether different. Her mind skittered through all sorts of possibilities involving bare broad shoulders, rumpled bed sheets and a lot more skin than he was showing now….

It kind of took her breath away.

It *was* her last night in St. Michel….

Even if he wasn't part of her "New Me" plan, she'd never see him again.

But then the strangest thing happened. Her better judgment kicked in.

What was the point of a one-night stand—besides a night of great sex?

Back home, her friend Ida May Higgins, the woman who'd known Lindsay since she was born, who'd cared for her after her mother died and had in many ways been a surrogate mother to her, insisted that the only way Lindsay could fix what her former fiancé, Derrick, had broken was by simply taking the time to be alone so that she could get to know herself.

Alone.

As in no one-night stands.

Besides, Sophie had yet to cut the cake and toss the bouquet. As the maid of honor, Lindsay needed to be available for Sophie, not formulating a plan to hook up with Mr. Hottie.

Willing herself not to look back at him, Lindsay swallowed the rest of her champagne, set the empty glass on a busing tray and made her way toward the terrace for a breath of fresh air.

Something—anything—to clear her head.

If she were at home right now, she'd pull out her mother's recipe book—a small red notebook filled with pages of handwritten recipes, mostly desserts—and bake. The kitchen was her sanctuary; baking helped her keep her sanity.

Even though she'd been so young when her mother had died she didn't have memories of her, she had her recipes. And bringing them to life somehow made Lindsay feel connected to this woman she never really knew.

She'd brought the red notebook to St. Michel with her but she hadn't been near a kitchen in the month she'd been there. So, since baking wasn't an option, she made her way toward the ballroom's open doors.

The terrace was dotted with a smattering of people. Mostly couples who'd stepped out into the moonlight for a little romance, it seemed, from the way people were paired up, some with arms entwined, others stealing little kisses—one couple, off in the far corner, getting a little too frisky for public decency.

Lindsay hated intruding on the romance, but she couldn't go back inside. Not just yet. To give them some privacy, she walked to the other end of the terrace, leaned against the ornate wrought-iron railing and tilted her face into the briny breeze that blew in off the ocean.

It was a gorgeous night. In North Carolina, she'd need a parka and gloves to be outside on a December evening. Here, the temperature was a little chilly, but it was brisk and fresh—just what she needed. She was already starting to feel revived.

After being in St. Michel a month, Trevard, North Carolina, seemed like a vague smudge on a distant horizon. It was hard to believe she'd be going home tomorrow. She blinked away the thought. No way would she waste her last night dwelling on the mundane. She'd have her fill of that soon enough.

She looked around, taking in the huge moon hanging over the water like a brilliant blood orange, spilling diamond seeds across the inky sky and into the restless sea below. Such a beautiful moon on Sophie and Luc's wedding night, as if the heavens were bestowing a special blessing upon their union.

It was all so romantic.

A shooting star burst across the sky like a Roman candle. Remembering her earlier conversation with Sophie, a chill skittered over her. She crossed her arms to rub away the goose bumps, then closed her eyes and wished…

When she was done, she looked around, blinking a couple of times at the couples paired up on the terrace.

Well, Cinderella, you're certainly not going to find your prince at Lover's Lane. Better get back inside.

As she turned to leave the happy couples to their romantic seclusion, she nearly bumped into someone. Backlit by the warm glow of the ballroom, he was silhouetted and she could barely make out his features. But she didn't need better light to recognize Carlos Montigo.

"It's a beautiful night," he said with a melodic Spanish accent, warming her from the inside out.

"It is beautiful. I was just—"

"If you're cold, I'd be happy to offer you my jacket."

"I appreciate the offer, but I'm fine."

He nodded and stepped up to the railing next to her. Looking at him from this angle made her draw in a quick breath. He might've been born of the bad-boy mold that attracted her, but something in his voice and in the way he carried himself suggested he was different. But exactly how, she couldn't discern.

"You made a beautiful bridesmaid for the princess."

"Thank you. Are you a friend of the bride or the groom?"

She cringed at the inane question. This was not North Carolina. Sophie hadn't met three-quarters of the guests, and she'd bet good money that Sophie and Luc didn't know most of them personally. That was what famous people did—hang out with other famous people. Go to their weddings. Whether they knew each other or not.

"I am acquainted with the Henri Lejardin, St. Michel's minister of art and culture, the brother of the groom. I have catered events for him in the past. I am in town for another occasion—the St. Michel Food and Wine Festival—and he invited me tonight.

"I am Carlos Montigo." He offered a hand and she took it.

"Lindsay Bingham," she returned.

He lifted her hand to his lips. She liked this gallant European custom.

His gaze slid to hers and locked into place.

An electric jolt coursed through her, and she couldn't look away. Even though she knew she should.

Oh, boy, she was in trouble.

But then, with the same air of rogue regality he'd shown when he so blatantly perused her from across the room, he released her hand and did a sweeping search of her face, his gaze finally lingering on her lips, which were suddenly so dry she had to moisten them before she could speak.

"Where are you from?" she asked.

"Florida."

"Really? I had you pegged for a European all the way."

"All the way?" he said, mimicking her slight southern accent. His mouth quirked up at the corner, forming a sexy half smile that Lindsay would've bet money had driven more than one woman wild.

"You're definitely American, and judging from the accent, from somewhere below the Mason-Dixon line. Am I right?"

"No, you're not. I don't have an accent."

He stood about a foot taller than Lindsay, yet now that her vision had adjusted to the moonlit terrace, she could see that his eyes were actually a deep shade of green rather than brown as she first thought.

"Yes, love, you do."

Oh, boy, indeed. Tall. Broad shoulders. Green eyes. A lethal trinity, and if she didn't watch herself, she could find herself in a lot of trouble. A cool breeze blew in across the water. She tipped her face up to it and closed her eyes, hoping it would help her regain her senses.

"Mmm, that's nice. Isn't it?"

"Paradise," Carlos murmured. "I think I may have just found paradise, Lindsay Bingham."

What?

"Really?" She leveled him with a bemused gaze. "And I think I've just heard the cheesiest pickup line ever."

They laughed, and his eyes did that face-searching thing again that made her feel completely and deliciously devoured.

"May I buy you a drink?" he asked. "Seeing that it's open bar."

"Only if it's the best champagne."

He smiled. "Wait right here. I'll be back. With a bottle."

She was definitely in trouble. Especially since in the five seconds that he'd been gone, she'd already begun to tell herself that Florida and North Carolina weren't that far apart. At least there wasn't an ocean between them.

Even so, it didn't mean she had to sleep with him just because the guy was coming on to her….

A little dose of harmless flirtation might be good for her. So why not?

Because.

That soothing breeze blew in again, caressing her. Not in a seductive way, but in a way that reminded her of her "New Me" plan.

In answer, she tipped her face into the breeze and breathed in deep.

Even though Carlos Montigo was tempting, she was tired. And if she was completely honest with herself, she didn't have the energy to play games. Because her gut was warning that if she laid one hand on the Montigo burner she would surely get burned.

"Lindsay? There you are."

It was Sophie. In that split second before Lindsay realized it, she'd checked her posture and smiled. Reflexive moves, thanks to the ever-present paparazzi that had been milling about the past month. Not because of how Carlos Montigo's gaze had just shamelessly undressed her, and in response she'd thanked him with her best *what happens on my last night in St. Michel stays in St. Michel* smolder….

Her cheeks burned, and she strengthened her resolve to resist temptation.

"I thought you were coming back?" Sophie said. "We've been looking for you." With her head, she gestured to Carson Chandler, who waited in the doorway. "Carson wants to talk to you."

Talk to me?

Sophie had introduced Lindsay to Chandler earlier that week. Tonight, as she and Sophie walked toward him, he'd acknowledged her with a polite, "Good evening, Ms. Bingham. Lovely to see you."

Why did he want to talk to her?

The billionaire media mogul had turned a travel guide business into an empire. Everyone knew his name. Sort of like how people *knew of* the Rockefellers or William Randolph Hearst.

Sophie gave Lindsay a look and mouthed, *surprise!*

"What?" Lindsay mouthed back.

But Sophie ignored her, turning instead to Chandler. "Carson, would you do me a favor?"

He smiled. "Certainly, your highness, your wish is my command."

"Will you dance with Lindsay? My *handlers* are beckoning." Sophie rolled her eyes and gave her head a quick shake. "Don't think I'll ever get used to having *handlers*. Or, for that matter, the fact that I need to be *handled*."

She turned on a flourish of tulle and silk, leaving Lindsay and the older man alone. There was an awkward pause during which Lindsay's mind spun. Carlos would be back any minute with the champagne. She couldn't just leave without excusing herself. What kind of surprise could Carson Chandler have for her? He was handsome in an aloof, moneyed way, but then again didn't all men look gorgeous in white tie? Still, he was old enough to be her grandfather. She resisted the urge to fidget, or worse yet, glance around for Carlos.

Finally, Chandler tilted his head to one side in a regal gesture and offered his arm. "Shall we?"

Feeling suddenly shy and exhausted, Lindsay tried to let him off the hook. "Please don't feel obligated to entertain me."

She was the kind of wrung-out tired that made even the thought of dancing feel like an effort. Since she was leaving tomorrow, what she really wanted to do was go upstairs and enjoy one last long, hot soak in that huge, marble tub in her suite.

"Dancing with you, Miss Bingham, would be my honor," said Carson. "Besides, I have something I need to talk to you about."

"Oh. Well, then." How could she deny a man his *honor?* One quick dance wouldn't hurt. In fact, she might even be back before Carlos returned with the champagne. "But please call me Lindsay."

She took his arm and walked back into the ballroom with him. When he smiled, he vaguely reminded her of Ricardo Montalbán sans accent. Of course he would. Because wasn't St. Michel *Fantasy Island?* How could she have missed that? A place where her best friend got to be a princess and Lindsay had been able to play Cinderella. For an entire month.

Here she was at the ball. Even though tomorrow her coach would turn back into a pumpkin and she'd board a plane homeward bound for Trevard, she'd had the time of her life.

Of course, she wished her Cinderella fantasy came with Prince Charming and happily-ever-after. But as

Carson Chandler whirled her around the gilded and mirrored ballroom, she glanced up at the crystal chandeliers, admiring the way the light played through the facets, illuminating the cut crystal like brilliant diamonds.

How many women got to attend a royal wedding in their lifetime? She should be grateful for the experience, even if the handsome prince didn't come chasing her across the Atlantic to see if the slipper fit.

Her gaze wandered back to the doors to the terrace. She wondered if Carlos was back yet. She hoped he didn't think she'd run out on him. Surely he'd wait. Wouldn't he? A ridiculous tangled sense of conflict flooded through her.

Oh, well. They'd just met and tomorrow she'd go home. Her "New Me" plan didn't call for leaving one Jimmy Choo behind on the palace step with the slim hope a man—even Carlos Montigo—would find it and bring it to her on the other side of the ocean.

"The princess tells me you've worked in television, Miss Bingham."

Carson's voice startled her back to the present.

"Excuse me?"

The orchestra was loud. She must not have heard him correctly. He leaned in closer. A little too close for Lindsay's comfort.

"You're such a beautiful woman. Actually, I haven't been able to stop thinking about you since we were introduced earlier this week. Princess Sophie tells me you have broadcast journalism experience?"

Her cheeks warmed and graceless dread unfurled in her belly, working its way up until it blocked the words to explain her short-lived journalistic career. The question unlocked a door in the recesses of her mind behind which she'd stashed a very bad memory. The memory of an incident that cost Lindsay her dream.

"I was curious about the type of television work you'd done?"

Sophie was one of the few people who knew of this thwarted dream. Why would she tell Chandler?

"I don't know what Sophie told you." *Or more important, why.* "But in college, I majored in broadcast journalism, and I reported for a network affiliate for a short time."

"Why for only a short while? I have a feeling the camera would love your face."

Lindsay stiffened, suddenly aware of his hand on the small of her back. Nothing improper, but now the door that had been closed tight for years had opened and a flood of bad memories…of a powerful man taking advantage…poured out.

"Relax, Miss Bingham, I didn't mean that the way it sounded. I'm a happily married man."

Okay.

She felt a little silly for jumping to conclusions. With her penchant for bad boys, obviously, she was no prude, but those relationships had always been mutual and consensual. Even if the men in her past had ended up being bad choices, she'd never sold herself for a job. And she never would. That's why she'd left the television industry in the first place.

"You didn't answer my question, Miss Bingham. Why are you no longer working in television?"

She wished she'd simply told him she had no experience rather than opening this can of worms. Oh, Sophie, what did you do?

"It just wasn't the career for me."

Again, his hand pressed into the small of her back as he gently led into a turn on the dance floor.

"Do you work now?" he asked.

She laughed. She couldn't help it.

"Well, yes. Of course I do. Not everyone here is royalty or independently wealthy."

Ugh, that sounded rude. She hadn't meant it to.

"I work for Trevard County Social Services in North Carolina. That's how I know Sophie."

"The same line of work as the princess's former job?"

"No. Not exactly."

"Well, what exactly do you do?"

She bristled. Why the game of fifty questions? She wasn't embarrassed by where she came from or that she'd chosen not to be a television talking head. She had an honest job. That was more than some could say—those who had no qualms about sleeping with a married man on their quest to the anchor desk.

"I'm the office manager."

"And do you enjoy your work, Miss Bingham?"

No.

"It's Lindsay." She glanced up at him, frowning. "Do you always ask so many questions, Mr. Chandler?"

"Only when I'm trying to decide if I'll invite someone to interview for a job."

A job?

The music stopped. Carson Chandler escorted Lindsay off the dance floor.

Wait! What job?

As they reached the edge of the parquet, he said. "Thank you for the dance. Miss Bingham, er, Lindsay, Chandler Guides produces a three-minute segment that airs on Food TV between full-length shows. It's called *The Diva Dishes.* The spots highlight travel, food and festivities of various destinations. Have you seen the spots?"

Lindsay nodded. She was addicted to Food TV.

"The *mini-sodes,* if you will, have the potential to boost the sales of our travel guides. But in the first year, increases didn't live up to our expectations. Because of that we let the host go. She didn't have that *diva* spark I was looking for. That *je ne sais quoi* that captivates."

He paused and put a hand to Lindsay's chin, looking her over appraisingly. "You really do have the most exquisite eyes, my dear. I'm sure everyone tells you so."

Lindsay's guard went up again like steel trapdoors. She was just about to pull away, a split second before Chandler dropped his hand.

"I digress," he continued. "Monday, right here in St. Michel, we will conclude auditions for the new host. The person we choose will start right away because we're taping this weekend at the St. Michel Food and Wine Festival. I'm inviting you to audition."

Every nerve in Lindsay's body went on hyperalert. The St. Michel Food and Wine Festival? Wasn't that the event Carlos mentioned?

But...but she couldn't audition. She was flying out tomorrow. Mary was expecting her back at work bright and early Monday morning. Plus, Chandler made her uncomfortable. Brought back too many bad memories.

He must have read the hesitancy in her expression, or perhaps she didn't return a properly enthusiastic response.

"Hundreds have auditioned, Lindsay. To be quite honest, you will be the only one we see Monday. I'm sure I needn't remind you that you have a fabulous friend in the princess. She was quite generous with her praise of you, and quite convincing that you are the diva for whom I've been searching."

An awkward pause followed this unexpected compliment. Boy, Sophie wasn't kidding when she said she had a *surprise.*

As Lindsay searched for how to respond to Chandler, the clock in the castle tower tolled midnight. Out of the corner of her eye, Lindsay glimpsed Carlos walk through the doorway that led in from the terrace, but then she lost sight of him as he was swallowed up by the crowd.

Chandler reached inside his breast pocket and produced a business card. In the style of a magician weaving a coin through his fingers, he presented it to her with a flourish.

"Call my assistant for the location of the audition. It will be a very nice, lucrative opportunity."

She took a deep breath, glancing around, trying to locate Carlos as she gathered the words she needed to nip Chandler's wild idea in the bud.

"Thank you for the offer, Mr. Chandler. I'm flattered, really I am. But it's been several years since I was in front of a camera. As tempting as the opportunity sounds, I'm afraid I'm not the person you're looking for."

"Oh, but I believe you are. Don't misunderstand, I'm not offering you the job on the spot." He smiled. "We'll have to see how you look on camera, but as I said earlier, I have a hunch the camera will love your face. And, Miss Bingham, my hunches are always right."

Chapter Two

"You left?" The vein in Max Standridge's forehead pulsed like it might explode. Normally, Carlos Montigo would rib him about it, but better judgment warned, *not today*.

Instead he settled into the hotel suite's couch, shrugged and pierced Max with his best *what of it?* stare.

Max pounded his fist once on the desktop. "You know the hoops I jumped through to wrangle you an invite to that wedding, Montigo. It was an opportunity, man. Why'd you leave? You could've at least made contact with the minister of art and education. We talked about how important that was."

"Why did I leave?" Montigo stood and grabbed the *La St. Michel* social page off the coffee table, took a few steps and flung it onto the desk. It careened across the glossy surface until Max stopped it with a slap of his palm.

"That's why I left."

He gestured to a front-page photo of Lindsay Bingham in her sexy red dress, wearing that drive-a-man-to-madness smile.

In the photo her arms were outstretched, the bridal bouquet was in midair, poised to fall gracefully into her elegant hands.

Max sneered. "You have something against brides tossing flowers?"

"Yeah, I'm a conscientious objector to weddings in general." Carlos rolled his eyes. "Especially when they toss the damn flowers eight times to get the right photo to con the world into buying the fairy tale wedding bull. What a crock of sh—"

"What does that have to do with anything?"

Max looked perplexed.

Carlos stared at the photo, into the eyes that had captivated him last night…at the face that had danced through his restless dreams making sleep fitful and his mood edgy because he was so damn tired today.

Max was his best friend, but there was no way Carlos could tell him that he'd narrowly escaped letting the woman get under his skin. But she'd ditched him while he went to get drinks, for a media mogul who could've bought and sold most of Europe.

Why should he be surprised that yet another woman followed the scent of money? Didn't they all?

If he told Max that, the guy would have license to mock him for a year, ribbing him about his bruised ego and poor choice of woman. So instead of fessing up, he improvised.

"It's fake," Carlos said. "The first toss hit her in the head. Nearly put her eye out. Since that wasn't the perfect *fairy tale* outcome, they did it again. And again. Eight. Times. It wasn't a wedding. It was a three-ring circus full of barracudas, phonies and opportunists."

Max pressed his hands to his eyes, then raked his fingers through his hair, pulling so tight that for a moment his eyes were drawn into slits. Carlos couldn't bear to look at him. So he turned around and reclaimed his spot on the sofa. The wedding had been closed to the paparazzi. The royal image makers were, no doubt, doling out the photos and video clips they wanted the world to see. How long would it take for the press to dig up the *real deal?* A rogue video or an embarrassing picture taken with a camera smuggled in by some opportunistic schmuck hungry to sell secrets?

"I'm your manager, Montigo, not a miracle worker. I can't help you if you won't help yourself."

Help me? He leaned back and laced his fingers behind his head.

"I'm not a charity case, Max."

"I didn't say you were, but you have to lose that chip on your shoulder if we're going to make this work."

For the love of God, the guy nagged more than Montigo's ex-wife, Donna.

The ornate hotel room with its frilly pink cabbage rose wallpaper was closing in on him. Just like the ballroom had last night. The only reason he didn't walk out right now was because Max, unlike Donna, hadn't walked out on him when the chips were down.

They needed one more good run.

Get in. Make money. Get out.

This cookbook needed to sell. Then Carlos could repay Max and use the rest for a project none of the beautiful people cared to touch.

Damn hypocrites.

And that was fine by him.

All he wanted was a restaurant where he could cook what he wanted to cook and play by his own rules. A place where he could open his doors to kids who'd screwed up and give them a fighting chance in this world.

Because didn't everyone deserve a second chance?

He'd had it all once—right in the palm of his hand. Until his fall from grace, when he'd lost everything.

The past two years had changed him. Rearranged his priorities. Proven that there were more important things than money and parties.

But it also showed him how much he valued his independence.

Now that the dust had settled and he'd begun to pick up the pieces, he knew he didn't need the pretty people to succeed. The ones who once called him friend, but now pretended to not remember his name. But that was fine—life in the fast lane came with too many strings and always, always too high a price.

He would make his own way—as he'd started to before Donna and all her glitzy ambitions. He would be beholden to no one.

"So I guess this means I need to cold-call Lejardin's office and try to get us in sometime in the next week," Max muttered, pensive, as if contemplating an impossible task.

"No need," Carlos said.

Max sighed, a weary, exasperated sound.

"Lejardin's stopping by the booth on Wednesday. Though you might want to call his assistant and confirm, things were pretty crazy at the wedding. They only had to do the garter toss six times. But still. Since he was in the wedding party, he was a little distracted. But I had to get out while I could. Before I hurt someone."

Carlos smiled at his own joke. Dazed, Max opened his mouth to say something, but nothing came out. He snapped his jaw shut.

Carlos reached inside his shirt pocket and pulled out a business card. "Here's his direct line. Should get you right through."

The trip to the airport where the St. Michel state jet awaited to fly Lindsay home to Trevard was a scenic fifteen minutes by limousine from the *Palais de St. Michel.* Lindsay settled into the soft leather seat, savoring her final glimpse of the St. Michel coast and the last vestiges of *the good life.*

Who knew when she'd return? She wanted to commit this parting scene to memory, to drink it all in. Even though she wanted to think she'd visit Sophie regularly, she didn't expect her friend to send a jet to fetch her every time they wanted a girls' weekend. And God knew she'd have to miser away every spare cent and every minute of vacation time before she could afford to take another trip abroad.

She sighed as they passed the yacht club, boats bobbing in the azure water, crisp, white sails billowing in the wind. Most of the vessels were larger than the modest apartment Lindsay called home.

Pointedly, she ignored the nagging question that kept forcing its way to the front of her mind—just how did one go back to Trevard after living like this?

Experts claimed it took twenty-one days to make a habit. She'd been here exactly thirty-two days. Not that it had taken anywhere close to twenty-one days to get used to the St. Michel life.

But the habit rule also worked in reverse, she reminded herself. She had a good job back in Trevard. A life there—no matter how much she'd love to stay in St. Michel, no matter how tempting Carson Chandler's offer to audition for *The Diva Dishes,* Lindsay had been away long enough.

The longer she put off going home, the harder it would be to go back. Besides, judging by the hoops she'd jumped through to get the time off—even though she had the vacation days—she didn't dare ask her boss for a single day more.

As the limo passed through a seven-story carved stone archway that resembled the *Arc de Triomphe,* a blue funk threatened to envelope Lindsay. She fought off the mood by reminding herself to look at the good. How many people had flown by private jet, been chauffeured by limousine and lodged in a five-hundred-year-old castle?

It was good while it lasted, and she needed to make the most out of these last moments rather than waste them brooding.

She grabbed her handbag, a cavernous Marc Jacobs—another bridesmaid gift from Sophie—and foraged for a compact and tube of lipstick to touch up her face before they arrived at the airport.

Instead of the makeup, her fingers found their way to Carson Chandler's business card and plucked it from the inner pocket where she'd stashed it. She ran her finger over the black letters embossed on the ivory-colored linen, then flipped it over and studied the bold script he'd used to write the contact number for his assistant, Sheila.

It would be a very nice opportunity for the right

person. And I believe you might be the right person, Miss Bingham.

Sophie had promised Chandler was a gentleman, "...happily married for nearly fifty years."

Interesting, since the man had a reputation in the business world for changing his mind as often as the wind changed directions. Even the spot he'd invited her to audition for seemed tentative.

"I'm not supposed to tell you this," Sophie had confided. "So you can't breathe a word, but you know he just purchased the Epicurean Traveler Network. Well, he wants to eventually turn the three-minute *Diva* spot into an hour-long show. You have to do this, Linds, because this little spot could turn into something really big."

Yeah, right. And it could be a dead end if he hired her and later decided to go with someone else—as he'd fired the previous Diva *host.*

Lindsay closed her eyes, trying to get Sophie's voice out of her head. "Cinderella certainly didn't get to the ball by locking herself away in the tower. She saw the opportunity and she took it."

Lindsay couldn't help but smile at the Cinderella metaphor. Wouldn't it be nice if life were simply one big fairy tale?

Then she wouldn't have to worry about cads who lied and cheated to get what they wanted.

Lies that cost Lindsay her fiancé, her job as a television reporter and her dignity.

"Chandler knows if he does you wrong he'll suffer the wrath of the future queen of St. Michel."

Lindsay sounded a humorless chuckle. God, Sophie almost sounded serious.

"Should I call you Ann Boleyn?" Lindsay had asked.

"*Nah.* Your royal highness will suffice." Then it was Sophie's turn to laugh. But her laugh was genuine. "You know I'm right, Linds. You've been hiding behind the reception desk. You're wasting your talent answering phones."

Really, when it came down to it, it wasn't the bad taste her foray into journalism left in her mouth as much as it was the uncertainty of the job in question.

Even if *The Diva Dishes* did have the potential to morph into a full-fledged television show, Chandler seemed too likely to change his mind midstream. His vision seemed too fickle. Sure, she had the future queen of St. Michel on her side—she still couldn't wrap her mind around the reality of Sophie's new life—but Chandler was a businessman and he'd make decisions based on what he deemed good for business, as evidenced by the way he fired the former host when she didn't live up to his expectations.

What if Lindsay couldn't pull it off? Her job at Trevard Social Services wasn't ideal, but she'd been there so long. It was comfortable—well, as comfortable as Mary Matthews allowed you to become. Lindsay's salary, though not huge, was enough to make ends meet, and you couldn't beat the government benefits.

Plus, she wouldn't be able to give two weeks' notice. Mary was certain to get her panties in a wad over that. She'd fussed over Lindsay taking time off for the wedding—even though Lindsay had more than enough accrued vacation.

No. Quitting on a whim just wasn't practical.

Sheila's number was one Lindsay wouldn't need, except for possibly making a courtesy *thanks-but-no-thanks* call.

An awkward uncertainty bubbled to the surface. Carson Chandler hadn't invited her to a party. So it wasn't as if she needed to RSVP, but he'd offered her a good opportunity. And she was the only one they were seeing at the St. Michel audition. Surely they'd have to arrange a camera ahead of time. It was rude to not call and tell them she wouldn't be there Monday.

The pang of missed opportunity pierced her, as she decided to call. If she'd learned one thing this month in St. Michel it was *when in doubt, err on the polite side.*

Lindsay pulled her cell phone out of the bag and switched it on. It had been off the entire week of the wedding when the battery had died, and she'd been too busy to worry about recharging it. She wasn't expecting any calls.

This morning, she'd remembered it needed charging and plugged it in, an afterthought as she prepared to leave. But she'd only bothered to turn it on now. And what she saw made her flinch: thirteen missed calls had gone to voice mail. All from her boss Mary Matthews over the past two days, Lindsay discovered, as she flipped through the call log.

Undistilled dread coursed through her as if someone had uncorked a bottle of something bitter and upended it into her system. *What did Mary want?* What was so darned urgent it couldn't wait until Lindsay was back in the office?

A multitude of possibilities sprang to mind, ranging from Mary wondering where she could find fresh file folders to her asking, "what's the phone number of that little sandwich shop that delivers?"

To Mary Matthews, a paper clip could be urgent if she couldn't put her fingers on one when she needed it.

Lindsay tapped a French manicured nail on the phone, debating whether to pick up the messages now or wait until tomorrow morning. When she was back on the clock.

After all, what could she do from this side of the Atlantic?

Tap. Tap. Tap. Tap.

But what if it *truly was* an emergency?

She struck the key that connected her to the voice mailbox.

The first message contained no greeting. No *I'm-sorry-to-bother-you-on-your-vacation-but* niceties.

It simply consisted of two words: "Call me."

After not hearing Mary's voice for so long, it was both familiar and strange, grating and startling in Lindsay's ear. It reminded her of how long she'd been away, and worse yet how she hadn't even missed home.

Not once.

The second call was a bit more forceful: "Lindsay, did you receive my message? I need you to call me."

Followed by: "Lindsay, this is the third time I've called. I don't understand why you're not returning my calls."

Which was followed by: "Lindsay, I am furious. We agreed you could take a month off as long as you remained available to me. You're not upholding your end of the bargain. Call me ASAP or—"

Lindsay clicked off the phone.

Call me ASAP or—or what?

How like Mary to call before Lindsay's vacation was over, assuming it would be no bother, no imposition to drop what she was doing and serve her.

Mary's voice had been adamant and crackling in that last call, like a live wire one wouldn't dare cross. But it was that call, that self-righteous tone of voice that suddenly shocked some sense into Lindsay.

Like a bolt out of the blue…

Shining a bright, hot spotlight on her cold, pathetic life.

This was what Lindsay was going back to. No family, a handful of lukewarm friendships, Mary Matthews and an unfulfilling office manager job that she'd fooled herself into believing was important. Rather than the dime-a-dozen job it was.

And if that realization wasn't enough, then…

She didn't waste time thinking about the consequences of ignoring this epiphany. As the limo driver turned left onto the runway access road that led away from the public portion of the airport back to the private hangars that housed the royal jet, Lindsay dialed the number Carson Chandler had written on the card.

Chapter Three

Never before had Lindsay landed a job *that* fast. After placing the call on Sunday, she went in the following day for a test taping. Now, here she was on Tuesday morning, standing amidst a maze of white tents that an army of workers were busily erecting on the St. Michel *Parc Fête* green.

She'd called Ida May, who had graciously agreed to continue looking after the house. And with that squared away, she was the new host of *Chandler Guide's Diva Dishes*. Rather than sitting behind the Trevard Social Services reception desk taking orders from Bloody Mary, she was on assignment at the St. Michel Food and Wine Festival.

Oh. My. God.

She shuddered as a giddy sense of possibility seemed as if it might lift her off the ground.

In the distance a symphony of hammers and power tools rang out a determined song. Drawing in a deep breath, she inhaled the scent of lumber, freshly mowed grass and the odor of the hard work that was happening all around her.

Tomorrow the place would be filled with epicures and delectable aromas from the various booths and cooking shows and demonstrations, but today the place more closely resembled a construction site.

Lindsay watched in wonder, trying to imagine how they would pull it off and have everything ready in time. Or, more aptly, tried to imagine how she would be ready for her first show by tomorrow.

She'd seen several of the previous *Diva* spots that had aired last year with the former host whom, Chandler proclaimed, came across like a cold fish. He was depending on Lindsay to breathe new life into the show, to deliver an edgier, more provocative performance that would boost recognition and sales of Chandler Guides. They were going for a younger, hipper image. And, he added, almost as an afterthought, he wanted her to be the sand in the oyster that produced a pearl. How was she supposed to accomplish that? By simply being herself, Chandler said.

Herself?

Edgy? Provocative? Gritty?

Oh, boy.

Quite frankly, the thought made her head spin. It felt as if she were on a wild ride, hanging on for dear life. She didn't dare loosen her grip or risk being flung out into the stratosphere. Only, for once in her life, she felt as if she just might be on a ride that would actually take her somewhere.

"There you are. Okay, here's what I've got." Paula English, *Diva Dishes* segment producer, rushed into the press tent, talking as she scribbled notes on a clipboard. The woman elevated multitasking to a new level. "We can talk with a French vintner or a local cheese maker…."

As her words trailed off, Paula frowned and gnawed her bottom lip, continuing to write notes to herself.

"Those are two of the most boring ideas I can think of," said cameraman Sam Gunn, who had trailed in behind Paula. Sam rounded out the three-member *Diva Dishes* team. It was a lean operation, and Paula pulled no punches upon their introduction when unsmiling, she sighed and said, "Oh goody. I get to train *another* new host." Then she promptly informed Lindsay that each person, *especially* Lindsay, was expected to pull his or her weight.

"There's no room for slacking and no time for learning curves," she'd said. "You'll have to hit the ground running if we're going to make our deadline."

Lindsay couldn't tell if Paula's brusqueness was simply business, or if it was passive-aggressive resentment toward the new girl.

Whatever. The vacation was over, and the pressure was on Lindsay to not only show Chandler he'd made the right choice in hiring her, but to prove to herself she hadn't made a fatal error by quitting her job back in Trevard.

"So that's all you've got?" Sam shook his head. "I hope to hell Lindsay is good at improvising because it's going to take a genius to make something brilliant out of that."

Improvised brilliance? A solid lump formed in Lindsay's throat, then it dropped like a lead ball into the pit of her stomach. Improvising had never been her strong suit. She'd learned late in the game that it was one of the things she hated about news reporting. Improvising meant saying the wrong thing. Embarrassing herself. She thought she'd outgrow the fear with a little experience under her belt. Her career had never made it to that point.

Paula lifted her gaze from the page and glowered at Sam. "Do you have a better idea?"

She didn't call him a moron, but her tone implied it. The tension between them was nearly palpable.

Sam arched a brow. "Last time I checked, I was the cameraman and you were the producer."

Sam gave Lindsay a conspiratorial wink that implied he was choosing sides. While it was good to have an ally in Sam, she didn't want the team to be divided. They had to work together or they'd go nowhere fast.

Paula tucked her pen behind her ear. "Quit heckling me and make yourselves useful."

She nodded at Lindsay. "Come on, let's go have a look around and see if we can come up with something better. Sam, you go scout locations."

Unsmiling, Sam stared at Paula long enough to raise the possibility of a showdown. But then he broke the standoff.

"This is your show," he said to Lindsay. "Don't let her push you around."

Paula frowned and looked as if she might spit nails. She hissed, "Meet back here at 5:30 p.m., Sam. We have a dinner meeting with Chandler."

Then Paula muttered under her breath as he walked away. Something that sounded suspiciously like, "That's why you don't sleep with your coworkers."

Lindsay's jaw dropped. "You and Sam?" The words fell out before she could stop them.

Paula turned her wary gaze on Lindsay and seemed to sum her up for a moment. Then, to Lindsay's surprise, Paula nodded. "Yeah. It was sort of messy. We were the inspiration behind Chandler Guide's Gunn-English policy."

"What?" Why was Paula telling her this?

"The Gunn-English policy." There was no warmth in her expression. "A *no fraternizing* policy."

Was this Paula's not-so-subtle way of saying hands off? Because it sure didn't feel like girl talk.

"*Ah,* thanks for the heads up," she said cautiously. She wasn't the least bit interested in Sam.

No way. No how.

She'd been through that before—she and her ex-fiancé, Joe, had worked at the television station—he'd been an up-and-coming anchor. She'd been a general assignment reporter. Their problems started when she confided in him about the uncomfortable advances their boss, Gerard Webb, was making when they were alone. After all, if you can't trust your fiancé, who can you trust?

But Joe shocked her by getting mad at *her,* saying "Don't blow it out of proportion, Lindsay, and most important, don't do anything stupid that will jeopardize our jobs."

How could she not say anything? How could he not stand up for her? But when it all hit the fan, Joe proved whose side he was on. When she filed the complaint against Webb, Joe broke off their engagement, claiming she must have been leading Webb on, doing something to give him the wrong impression. In other words, she "must have asked for it."

"There's no sense in the two of us staying here," Paula said. "I'm going to go talk to the festival coordinator. You stay here." She gestured to a table full of literature on the far side of the tent. "See if you can find something better for the show in the press kits."

Then without so much as a goodbye, Paula turned and walked away, leaving Lindsay on her own.

It was make-it-or-fall-flat-on-her-face time. Since the latter wasn't an option, she had to get her rear in gear. The best place to start was to find a knockout idea for the first show, proving that she could pull her weight.

Dodging a team of men hauling a stack of boxes, she made her way to the publicity table. She scanned the various brochures, press kits and photos stacked neatly on the cloth-covered rectangular table. A familiar face snagged her gaze. Smiling up at her from a photo pasted on the cover of a blue folder was none other than Carlos Montigo.

Lindsay's stomach performed an erratic somersault that drew a defensive hand to her belly.

With her free hand, she reached for the folder.

The press kit was printed on glossy paper. No expenses spared. Impressive. It had all the makings of a staged comeback.

Lindsay opened the folder and pulled out a bio, which gave the general who—Carlos Montigo; what—self-taught chef; when—he'd been cooking all his life; where—born in Madrid, raised in Paris, and subsequently made his mark after he moved to Miami; and why—because food was his passion, *yada yada yada*. But no mention of his hiatus.

Of course not.

Behind the bio was one of his signature recipes for

beef bourguignonne and several eight-by-ten glossy black-and-whites: Montigo working in a restaurant kitchen; Montigo on the set of a cooking show; Montigo smiling warmly and toasting the camera with a glass of wine. Good photos of a gorgeous man—longish, glossy dark hair. Great bones that the camera loved. The trademark dark stubble on his jaw that made him look ruggedly handsome, but there was something about his crooked nose and the look in his eyes that promised danger. Good lord, the man made her squirm, and if there was one thing she couldn't resist it was a man who made…a good subject for the third *Diva Dishes* segment.

Lindsay had been out of the television business for several years, but despite advances in technology, one truth remained: a good reporter did her research before an interview.

She had a lot to learn about Carlos Montigo, and what she learned this afternoon—without letting his sexy smile and rugged good looks cloud her judgment—would tell her whether she'd pitch the story to Carson, Paula and Sam.

Sure, *The Diva Dishes* wasn't *60 Minutes,* but her gut told her there was a story here, and she was bound and determined to have a meaty idea to present to them at five-thirty.

So, she went back to the hotel and booted up the MacBook Chandler had given her when she accepted the job.

Leaning back against a stack of pillows, she performed a Google search of Montigo's name. One hundred fifty thousand matches came up.

The first listing was a *Wikipedia* entry. She clicked on it and the page opened, revealing a color photograph of Carlos that made her bite her bottom lip. Underneath the photo it said:

Carlos Montigo is a restaurateur and celebrity chef. The former owner of South Miami Beach's Prima Bella Donna starred in one season of Food TV's You Want A Piece of Me?

He was born in 1972 in Madrid, Spain and raised in Paris, France. He moved to Miami, Florida after meeting Donna Lewis and together, the two opened Prima Bella Donna. The couple divorced in 2006 citing irreconcilable differences. Lewis is now sole owner of the restaurant and has employed three different chefs in the two years since Montigo has been gone.

Montigo was the center of controversy when a reporter for the Miami Herald *initially set out to write a story about Montigo's refusal of a Michelin star and in the process discovered that the chef had lied about his credentials.*

Following the exposé, Food TV terminated Montigo's contract on the show You Want A Piece of Me.

Lindsay blinked. He lied? Why on earth would a man who was seemingly sitting on top of the world fake his credentials?

She scrolled down to a list of resources the author used for the story. She found a link to the *Miami Herald* story and clicked on it.

Miami Herald *February 10, 2006*

Celebrity Chef Spices Up Resume

Carlos Montigo, the celebrity chef/owner of Prima Bella Donna in South Beach, who rose to fame on the wings of the Food TV show You Want a Piece of Me *has caught his pants-on-fire. It seems Montigo, 35, falsely positioned himself as a culinary hotshot with hoity-toity credentials. In response, Food TV executives have relieved him of the remainder of his contract. They will show reruns of the episodes that have already been taped.*

According to Montigo's biography on FoodTV.com the chef claimed to hold a diploma from the prestigious Le Cordon Bleu culinary arts school in Paris. Au contraire, say school officials. "Our records cannot substantiate a connection between Monsieur Montigo and the school. He did not earn a Grand Diplome from our institution and should cease and desist connecting himself to Le Cordon Bleu."

Also, he maintained he was formerly a chef at the Élysée Palace in Paris, the official residence of the French president. That assertion also was proven to be a lie.

Montigo and his representatives did not return phone calls before the publication of this article.

It was like reading about a train wreck. What would possess him to do that? How did he think he could get away with falsifying his background? When you're in the public eye, you're begging people to ask questions and snoop around. Well, that's exactly what she'd ask him tomorrow when they met.

Her conscience protested.

It would be awkward digging up the past, rehashing things he probably wanted to put behind him—asking the tough questions was another aspect she'd found difficult about journalism.

She stared at the black-and-white photo of Carlos on the screen, a shot of Carlos in a leather jacket and a tough look on his handsome face, a publicity shot for *You Want A Piece of Me.*

But surely if he was promoting himself at the festival he had to know that media would ask questions.

She'd have to. It was her job—especially since Chandler wanted edgy.

Well, as edgy as you could get in a three-minute spot.

She searched some more and viewed Carlos's Web site, which was all about pitching his new cookbook—published by Lone Wolf Press.

Hmm...never heard of that house.

It also had recipes and a bio that didn't reveal anything new. It only mentioned his brief relationship with Food TV and his old stomping ground, Prima Bella Donna, in passing.

Nothing about the controversy.

The Food TV site was even less revealing. There was no mention of Carlos Montigo. It was as if he'd never existed in their realm.

She searched hundreds of articles that appeared in her Google search, but they were simply rehashings of the *Herald* article and didn't offer anything new.

Until she clicked on one that showed Carlos and a attractive brunette toasting each other on a Mediterranean-styled terrace with a gorgeous water view behind them.

The title of the article, which was presumably written before all hell broke loose, was *The Chef and His Prima Donna.*

Lindsay skimmed it, wanting to know more about this woman who, according to the article, was no wallflower, and what caused their irreconcilable differences.

They looked so happy in the photo.

According to the article, equal parts of Carlos's cooking and her charm were responsible for growing their Prima Bella Donna into the toast of the South Beach restaurant scene.

So this was his ex.

Lindsay studied her pretty face and the way Carlos was smiling at her. It reminded her of the way that Luc looked at Sophie.

But no! That was completely different.

Sophie and Luc were happy.

Carlos and Donna were…divorced.

Does love ever last?

How do you go from looking at each other as though the sun rose and set in your love's eyes to being…irreconcilable?

She blinked away the thought. She had just opened a word processing program on her computer and began to write notes and interview questions when her cell phone rang.

"Hello?"

"Lindsay? It's Sophie. How are you?"

Thrilled at the sound of her friend's voice, Lindsay sat up. She set the laptop aside and swung her feet over the side of the bed.

"Sophie, hi! It's so good to hear your voice, but why on earth are you calling me? You're on your honeymoon."

Sophie laughed. "Are you kidding? Do you think I could wait another two weeks to see how your meeting with Carson went? Besides, Luc went down to consult with the concierge about a trip we want to take tomorrow. So I have a few minutes. Tell me how it went."

For a split second, Lindsay considered playing a joke on Sophie—like they used to kid each other when they worked together—she thought about saying she'd gone home without talking to Chandler…or better yet, that Chandler said, "Thanks, but no, thanks." But she didn't have the heart. Not when her friend had been so good to give her this opportunity, and she didn't want to waste the precious little time they had to talk playing a prank.

"He offered me the job."

Sophie squealed. "And?"

"And we start shooting tomorrow at the St. Michel Food and Wine festival. In fact, I was working on my interview questions. Oh, Sophie, I don't know how I will ever repay you for this."

"You can repay me by knocking the socks off Chandler…and your admiring public."

"No pressure, huh? Couldn't I just take you to lunch the next time I see you?"

They both laughed.

"Lunch would be good. Could we set a date for a return visit now?"

Lindsay sighed. "I wish we could, but with work, I don't know when I'll be able to make it back to St. Michel."

"Oh, Linds, I'm so happy for you. Not to bring up a sore subject, but how did Mary take it? I'll bet she had a fit."

Lindsay sighed. "That's putting it mildly. I thought she was going to reach through the phone and strangle me. I've never quit a job without giving at least two weeks' notice."

Lindsay cringed at the thought.

"Right, but she should understand you're not just ditching her. This is the opportunity of a lifetime."

"I hope so because if not, I've just blown years of my life because Mary informed me she won't give me a good reference—no way, no how."

"Well, you won't need one. Despite my prodding, Carson wouldn't have chosen you if he didn't see something special in you, Linds."

"Here's my idea." Lindsay took a deep breath and placed Carlos Montigo's press kit on the restaurant table in front of Carson Chandler. She, Paula and Sam were having dinner with Carson to firm up their game plan for the first show.

They still hadn't ironed out the focus of the show. When they met back at the press tent, Lindsay, giddy with possibility, had spouted her idea. Even though she'd anticipated Paula being a hard sell, Lindsay had no idea that woman would be so disagreeable and dead set on her wine and goat cheese man.

It was clear that Paula was turning the show content into a competition when she grabbed the first opportunity to present her idea to Chandler—before they'd even been seated at the restaurant.

Chandler had nodded politely, and asked as they walked to the table, "But where's the edginess in wine and goat cheese, Paula? Remember, we're making the jump from run-of-the-mill to edgy and provocative."

When Paula didn't reply, Lindsay decided it was time for her pitch. She took a deep breath and twisted her hands into the napkin on her lap.

"Do you remember that Food TV chef, Carlos Montigo?" Lindsay asked. "The one who got the boot because he lied about his credentials? Well, he's here at the festival and it looks like he's staging a comeback."

Paula grimaced as she opened the menu. "Why would you want to give him free press?"

"It's not free press," Lindsay said. "It's a chance to

give Carson the type of story he wants. Something with an edge."

Lindsay glanced at Chandler to gauge his response, but he was staring at the menu. She wasn't sure if he'd heard her. If he had, he didn't look enthused.

Over the menu, Paula regarded Lindsay with arched brows and a smug smirk that gave her pessimistic mouth an ironic upturn. No backing there—no surprise. So, Lindsay looked to Sam for support, but he was busy buttering a dinner roll. For a moment, an awkward silence enveloped them.

Okay.

She took a deep breath, inhaling the delicious aroma of herbed bread baking in a wood-burning oven. The enticing scent of rosemary and thyme filled the restaurant and fueled her courage. Giving the napkin one last twist, Lindsay decided it was time for the new girl to prove her mettle.

"In all my research, I couldn't find anything telling his side of the story," Lindsay said. "This is a chance to ask him *why* he lied and to hear about his future plans."

Paula closed her menu and shook her head, as if Lindsay had proposed a feature on *The Wiggles* or something else laughably inappropriate and ridiculous.

"Who cares?" Paula choked on an incredulous laugh, then pursed her lips as if stifling the urge to guffaw. She looked at Chandler as if she expected him to have the same reaction.

"Who cares?" Lindsay countered. "A lot of people would find the story interesting."

"Maybe we can catch up with him for another episode," Paula dismissed. "Since we're in St. Michel, we'll go with the wine and goat cheese theme."

Chandler held up his hand. “Not so fast, Paula. You haven’t made a case for your goat man.”

Paula laughed again, as if she expected Chandler to join in on the joke. But his serious expression warned otherwise.

“I think Lindsay is onto something with the Montigo story,” he said. “Let’s move forward with it.”

Chapter Four

Carlos's role in the food and wine fest was three-fold and simple: He'd host a one-hour, audience-interactive cooking demonstration; join five chefs in presenting a charity fundraiser "celebrity chef" dinner; and sign books at a launch party celebrating the release of his new cookbook, *Carlos in the Kitchen.*

The launch party, sponsored by the publisher, Lone Wolf Press, was his last event in the lineup. And, by all accounts, the most important to him.

There was a lot riding on this book.

As the taxi stopped in front of the Hotel St. Michel, Carlos tucked a copy of the new cookbook under his arm.

No one need know that Carlos and Max were the driving force behind Lone Wolf. It wasn't ideal to self-publish and throw a party for himself. But his former publisher had dropped him and these days corporate sponsors were hard to come by.

The way he and Max had sheltered the publishing house, no one need be the wiser. Right now, that was the last thing on his mind. Things were off to a great start. Max, who deserved a huge bonus once they got on their feet, had secured an interview with the new host of *The Diva Dishes.* That interview was the reason he'd rushed back to the hotel.

Now, as he stood in front of the door to the hotel suite he shared with Max, he raked a hand through his hair and took a moment to get his head in the game before he entered the room.

He'd thought a lot about what Max had said about losing the chip on his shoulder and he supposed his friend was right. Sometimes Carlos could be his own worst enemy. He'd lived a desolate, flatlined life since his fall from grace.

That's what caused his career to self-destruct. Now that he'd quit feeling sorry for himself and was trying to rebuild his life, he could either go with the flow or make it an uphill, and quite possibly losing battle. He might be proud, but he wasn't stupid.

This was an opportunity, a means to an end. He would go in there and charm the media into an endorsement.

He practiced a smile, which felt tight and insincere at first, but gradually eased into something that felt like a pleasant expression. One more deep breath, then he opened the door.

Okay. Showtime.

"Carlos, my man." Max stood and spread his arms wide. Yep. Nothing said *showtime* like Max in amped-up PR mode. "Come in. Come in. We've been waiting for you."

He hadn't even closed the door behind him when his gaze locked on the blonde sitting on the couch.

Lindsay Bingham?

What the—

Only, today she wasn't swathed in the low-cut, curve-hugging gown that had mesmerized him Saturday night. She'd traded it in for a sleek black, knee-length skirt and white button-down blouse that should've spelled sensible, but on her it looked even sexier than that gown that had been cut to places that might've been illegal in some cultures. Her long, straight, blond hair was loose today, framing her face. He tried not to stare at the way her skirt was hitched up over her knees—rather pretty knees at that, and long, slender legs that were enough to drive a man to distraction.

What was she doing here?

There were few things that Carlos hated more than being caught off guard. Unpredictability was one of the things he hated most about being in the limelight. He wanted to follow the script—like an old reliable recipe—but invariably surprises sprang up.

He hated surprises.

So why was it that underneath the *surprise* of finding this unpredictable woman in his hotel room, he was happy to see her?

Carlos walked over to the party of five gathered in the living area and placed the cookbook on the coffee table, front and center.

"I'd like to introduce you to the crew of Chandler Guides's *Diva Dishes,*" said Max. "This is Carson

Chandler, CEO of Chandler Guides and the show's executive producer."

"Carlos Montigo," he said, shaking Chandler's hand. For the first time since he'd seen Lindsay with Chandler at the wedding, he felt a surge of possibility. Pieces were starting to click into place. He hadn't considered the possibility that Lindsay's relationship with Chandler might be strictly business. Experience—Donna, his mother—had proven more often than not most women followed the money.

"This is *Diva* cameraman, Sam Gunn," Max continued, "Segment Producer Paula English, and Lindsay Bingham, the show's new host."

Lindsay held out her hand and dazzled him with a smile. Even wearing muted tones, she looked impossibly brilliant against the room's prim floral motif. As if her energy claimed physical space.

"I believe we've met," he said, taking her hand.

"Yes, we have," she said. "You disappeared the other night. I didn't get to say good-night."

Her skin was as soft as he remembered, and her handshake firm, yet every bit as feminine as he thought it would be. Since Saturday, visions of this woman had lingered in his mind. Without warning, that face—with those haunting brown eyes, those full, tempting lips—had randomly popped into his thoughts, leaving him vaguely wanting and unsettled.

And here she was standing in front of him. Again.

Did she have her manicured fingers in every newsmaking pie in St. Michel? Maid of honor to the princess. Headline-grabbing bouquet catcher. Chandler Guides's brand-new Diva.

Whatever the case, he was glad to see her. Because,

of course, he wanted to be sure the diva worked her magic promoting *Carlos in the Kitchen.*

"Here's a copy of Carlos's itinerary for the duration of the Festival." Max handed each of them each a crisp white sheet of paper.

"How did you want to do the interview?" he asked. "Do you want to start here or on location?"

The *Diva* crew glanced at the papers.

"The segment will only be three minutes," Paula said in a slightly irritated deadpan. "We want to shoot during his audience-interactive cooking demonstration. His show's scheduled for two o'clock. We'll meet you backstage at one o'clock."

"No preliminary interview?" Carlos asked.

"No time," Paula answered.

"But we'll get to see the script first, right?" Max asked.

Though Carlos didn't think it was possible, Paula's face hardened even more. "We don't use a script. We wing it."

There was something about that woman he didn't trust. Something about her that didn't sit right. He took people at face value now. Because of Donna, he didn't make excuses for anyone anymore. He heeded his gut's warning. With his ex-wife, he'd brushed off *this,* made allowances for *that.* In the end, Donna had made a fool of him. He'd seen it coming, yet he'd sat back and let her have her way until she'd systematically ruined his life.

He had no one to blame but himself. But one thing was for damn sure: it would never happen again.

"I'm not comfortable with winging it," Carlos said. "So, thanks for your interest, but I can't help you with your show."

Max shot him a *what-the-hell-are-you-doing?* look as Carlos turned to walk out of the room.

"What Paula means," Lindsay interjected, "is that we take an *organic* approach when we film. Tomorrow, we'll play off the audience, talk about what you're cooking and go with the general mood of the show. No worries. I promise."

Carlos stopped, his back to the *Diva* crew and considered her words for a moment. Why should he trust her any more than the woman she worked with?

"I have an idea," Chandler offered. "Why don't we have dinner tonight? We can get to know each other. You know, break the ice before tomorrow."

Carlos turned. "No. I don't want a group get-together, but I will reconsider if Lindsay will agree to have dinner with me. If we have too many cooks in the kitchen, it'll be counterproductive. Since she'll be interviewing me, we're the ones who should meet."

The Rivera Ivoire on the Boulevard St. Michel was an intimate jewel of a restaurant. It wasn't a three-star establishment, but it had a solid reputation for stellar food. It was one of his favorites. So it was the only possible choice for dinner with Lindsay. Not to mention, here he didn't know the chef and that was fine with him.

Despite his reputation as the outcast who'd lied about his credentials, two years out of the game, few industry professionals acted like they recognized him. Of course, that meant no chef-to-chef professional courtesies. But he wasn't looking for special treatment. In fact, he preferred to remain anonymous.

Carlos stood when Lindsay walked into the dining

room, lighting up the place like sunshine through gray clouds. More than one head turned as she walked by.

She looked bohemian in her flowing cobalt-blue skirt, gauzy white peasant top and brocade shawl. Still graceful and beautiful, but staggeringly different from the elegant socialite in red who'd caught the princess's bridal bouquet—and his eye. And different yet again from the businesswoman who'd appeared in his suite earlier today.

The woman was a jumble of contradictions, and the sight of her as she walked toward him made him smile despite himself.

The way she carried herself with her long hair swinging loose about her shoulders made her look like a gypsy. *Maybe she'd bring him good fortune?*

Yeah, right. How could he even contemplate such crap? She was here to get a story, and he needed to make damn sure he steered the direction that story would go.

She smiled as she walked toward him, and he could've sworn sparks ignited the instant their eyes met.

"Sorry I'm late." She offered him her hand. He held on to it and gazed at her, happier to see her than good sense warranted.

"I got tied up going over the camera shots with Sam." She pulled her hand from his. "Time got away from me, but it's going to be a great spot."

"No problem." He pulled out a chair for her, and she sat. "I haven't been waiting long."

Her bracelets chimed as she pushed her long hair over her shoulder, no doubt sizing him up as he took his seat across the table from her; reconciling the man before her with the cad the news stories had concocted.

Hell, everyone he met looked at him that way these days, since his life hit the fan and the intimate details of who he was or, more important, who he *wasn't,* flew out into the open for all to judge.

Still, even though the media had burned him, to get what he wanted, he needed some good press to turn his ship around. That was the only reason he was going through with this interview on *The Diva Dishes.*

He picked up the open bottle of wine and poured some for her.

"This is a Chateau Troplong Mondot Saint Emilion 2000. I hope you like red."

"I do," she said. "Thank you."

He handed her the goblet and touched his to hers.

"Here's to a good show."

"Cheers," she said, and lifted it to her full lips, sipped, then considered her glass. "I thought you said you hadn't been waiting long?"

He shook his head as he savored the classic, rich berry, cherry and spice of the full-bodied wine. "It needed time to breathe before we enjoyed it."

She grinned. "You haven't been waiting long, yet you had ample time to order and aerate a bottle of Saint Emilion—and quite a nice one, I see."

With his forearms resting on the edge of the table, he toyed with the knife at his place setting. "So maybe I was early. You caught me."

She clucked her tongue and tsk-tsked. "Punctuality is such a bad habit. You really should do something about it."

She smiled warmly, a glint of mischief sparkling in her brown eyes. He was suddenly very glad they were dining together.

After officially meeting Carlos Montigo in his hotel suite earlier that day, Lindsay's first impression was that he was an egomaniac—wanting to dictate the direction of the show, and threatening to pull out when things didn't go his way.

But as they ordered and Carlos gradually let down his guard, he seemed…charming. Before talking to him, she would've expected a Muzak orchestra to break into a chorus of "You're So Vain" when he walked into a room.

Now she was willing to give him the benefit of the doubt. Maybe she'd misjudged. Either the tabloids were wrong or the man was a veritable Jekyll and Hyde. Even though there was usually a grain of truth in tabloid headlines, she'd certainly never placed much stock in them. Never had a reason to until now. They were just something to look at in passing. Something to read and secretly roll her eyes at as she waited in the checkout line at the supermarket.

But now that she'd met Carlos, the truth suddenly mattered. That was what she intended to get to the bottom of tonight.

The conversation flowed naturally and fluidly. Mellowed by the wine and lulled by his silken, slightly-European accent—Spanish tempered by his years in France and the States—she was swept up in the ebb and flow of his voice as he candidly talked about his early years in Spain and France; how he learned to cook in his grandmother's kitchen—nothing she didn't already know from her research, but it was interesting hearing it from him.

It was strange knowing so much about someone she'd just met. It almost felt a tad stalkerish, but it was all in a day's work. It was her job to do be well-informed and armed with pertinent questions.

"What happened with Food TV, Carlos?" she asked.

She could almost see the wall going up around him. It was a physical shuttering of the sexy, funny man who'd beguiled her with candid tales of his early years.

"I'm sure you know the story. You've done your homework."

"Yes, I have." She toyed with her bracelet before looking up at him. "Over and over again, I read the same account of how you falsified your credentials. But nowhere did I read your side of the story. How come, Carlos?"

His expression was impassive. Yep, the wall was firmly in place. And it was steely and cold.

"For the interview, I'd prefer to look forward, not back."

"But you've never told your side of the story. Why?"

He smiled without warmth and shook his head, then looked down into his wineglass and gave it a swirl. "What good would that do? The media has already told the story it wants to tell. If I offered a rebuttal two years after the fact, it would do nothing but open old wounds. After all this time, it's old news. There's no sense in rehashing that can of worms. However, I would like to focus on what the future holds."

Ugh. Okay. Fine. He wins.

She'd always been bad at asking the hard questions. That was one of the excuses that Gerard Webb had used for firing her.

She certainly wasn't going to sit here and fight with him. Because even then she wasn't sure he'd trust her with the information. Extracting the truth out of an interviewee just wasn't her strong suit. That's why she wasn't a good journalist.

She sighed inwardly.

"So what does the future hold for Carlos Montigo?"

"I'm getting back to my roots. I haven't been to St.

Michel in ten years, and now here I am touring Europe—at least for now—promoting my cookbook. Life is good, Lindsay. It'll be even better when I can return to my house in Cedar Inlet. But for now, I'll enjoy St. Michel and the company of a gorgeous woman."

He raised his glass to her, and the way he looked at her left her strangely breathless, but if she stuck to her mental list of interview questions, she'd get over it.

"What about South Beach?" Lindsay asked. "Do you miss it?"

A smile tugged at the corners of his mouth, but it didn't reach his eyes. He took a slow sip of wine as he pondered the question.

Finally, he said, "I don't miss it a bit. Not a single thing about it."

"Why did you pass on the Michelin star?" She held her breath, aware that he'd never gone on record answering that question.

For an awkward moment Carlos didn't answer, and she feared that he wouldn't.

"Again, I'd rather not dwell on the past, but if you promise me this is off the record...give me your word that tomorrow these questions won't be part of the interview, I'll tell you."

Her heart pounded against her rib cage. "Of course."

He regarded her warily. "I would've sacrificed a lot of my freedom in exchange for those stars. Since I was away from the restaurant more than I was there, it seemed to be better for the restaurant for me to pass on the honor."

"In other words it would've been too much pressure to keep up?" she asked.

Carlos shrugged, pulling that impassive look again.

"Interesting. Your trying to keep your freedom was exactly what led to the media investigation that robbed you of all you'd worked so hard to build?"

Another awkward moment flared. Only this time, it soon became clear, as Carlos crossed his arms over his chest, he had no intention of answering the question.

Whatever had passed between them earlier had evaporated. "Earlier, you mentioned Cedar Inlet, Florida. I'm not familiar with it. How is it different from South Beach?"

Carlos chuckled and she was relieved he seemed to have loosened up again. "They're like black and white," he said. "Day and night. One is all about glitz and money, seeing and being seen. The other is natural and laid-back—it works with your rhythms, whereas you have to get in tune with South Beach rather than it synching with you. You see, I have this dream that—"

He stopped and shook his head as if he'd caught himself in the nick of time.

"A dream?" she asked. "Go on."

"It's not important."

"Dreams are always important. Sometimes they're the only thing that keep us sane."

"I understand that, what I meant is that it's not important that I share that information with you."

His words crashed down like a wave pulling her under for a moment, then spitting her out, disoriented, on the shore. He must have read the bewilderment on her face, because he said, "That was rude. I apologize. What I meant is it's not relevant to our interview and I'd rather focus on the cookbook."

She shrugged. "Maybe the next time I interview you, it will be about that dream."

* * *

He wasn't trying to be rude, not on purpose, though he could be when it served him. He hadn't expected the flash of hurt on her face when he steered the conversation back around to the purpose of this dinner. Maybe Lindsay Bingham was more human than media automaton after all.

A curious thrill shot through him. He couldn't quite figure her out, but one thing was certain, she was one hundred percent woman—a smart, funny, richly complex woman. Someone he definitely wanted to know better.

The waiter brought the bill, and Carlos reached for his wallet.

"Mr. Chandler has already taken care of the tab." Lindsay smiled triumphantly. "This is just a receipt."

He sat back in his chair.

"Thank you, but it wasn't necessary," Carlos said. "When I invite a woman to dinner, I pay. Business or not."

His words, *business or not,* seemed to reverberate in the ensuing silence. They begged the question—*was this business...or not?* Because somehow suddenly the mood had shifted, the air between them seemed charged and for a reckless moment, he wanted to trust her, wanted to open up and share.

"Come on, let's get out of here," he said. "I want to show you something. Do you feel like taking a walk?"

"Sure," she said tentatively. "Where to?"

He gave her his warmest smile, taking in the alluring contrast of her dark eyes and her pale blond hair. "It's a surprise."

They stood. She grabbed her handbag, and he helped her with her wrap.

Soon they found themselves out in the chilly night air walking past the casino through streams of well-dressed people, toward the beachfront park.

"So what's it like being Chandler's new Diva?" he asked as they walked.

A Diva? Me?

She decided to not take the question literally.

"Actually, this is my first show. I've had the job for all of three days."

"Really? What did you do before?"

And as they made their way along the ancient cobblestone street that led through the heart of downtown St. Michel, Lindsay regaled him with the story of how, with a little nudge from her good friend the princess of St. Michel, she'd landed the position as the show's host.

Amusement lit his eyes. "You must lead a charmed life to stumble upon a job like this."

She shrugged. "Hardly, but I am fortunate to have such a good friend as Sophie. I wouldn't be here right now if not for her. Now, if you want to talk about someone leading a charmed life, she's the one."

A strange sense of irony tugged at her insides. Yes, indeed, if not for Sophie, Lindsay *wouldn't* be here right now in St. Michel, walking with this gorgeous man, feeling as if anything were possible.

Maybe some of Sophie's charm had rubbed off, Lindsay thought as she stole a quick glance at Carlos. His profile wasn't perfect, which was reassuring. His nose was slightly too big and there was a bump on the bridge that made it a little crooked—but that simply added to his charm.

They walked in comfortable silence for a few minutes, listening to the *whoosh* of cars whizzing by, intermittently muting the conversations of giddy passersby en route to the casino and various clubs and restaurants that lit up the Boulevard St. Michel.

It was so intimate walking with him, the two of them together, making their way through the throngs of people. They walked so close, yet didn't touch. That made her all the more aware of him. It was as though she could feel the heat radiating off him, beckoning her closer.

"So, a man who cooks," Lindsay said, feeling suddenly brave. "Why hasn't some lucky lady snapped you up? Unless someone already has?"

She hadn't thought of that until now. Nothing had been written about him since the initial media nightmare about losing the show and his divorce. Maybe he'd found someone. But that would be part of the story, and it was her job to ask questions like that—for the story.

"There's been no one recently I've wanted to be involved with."

His answer made Lindsay bite her lip. "Oh, I'm sorry."

Sort of.

"We've talked about me all night," he said. "Tell me about you."

She tucked a strand of hair behind her ear.

"Talking about *you* was the purpose of the dinner," she said.

He pinned her with a devastatingly persuasive look, and something in the way his eyes crinkled at the corners when he smiled made her happy he wanted to know about her.

"Well, let's see…I was born and raised in Trevard, North Carolina. This trip to St. Michel is my first trip out of the United States."

"Really? You seem so worldly."

"Worldly? Somehow that doesn't sound like a compliment."

"Oh, but it is." He winked at her. "At the wedding, I had you pegged as a jet-setter. You know, one of the beautiful people."

She smiled and ducked her head a little, embarrassed.

"So you must like Trevard to have stayed there so long?"

She shrugged. "Life sort of dictated my staying put."

"Really?"

She nodded. "My mother died when I was young. It was just my father and me for so long. I guess felt a little responsible for him. Especially since I never really knew my mother." She glanced up at him to gauge his reaction, unsure if she'd said too much. But the warmth in his eyes spurred her on. "All I have of her is her old recipe book. It's this little red notebook. All the recipes are handwritten. I've always had this crazy notion that if I could master all those recipes, I might know her somehow…."

She gave her head a slight shake, wishing she hadn't said it.

"I'm sure that sounds ridiculous. Just—" She waved her hand, as if she could erase the comment. He wasn't interested. He was just being polite.

He shook his head. "Why would that sound ridiculous? I think you can tell a lot about a person through the things they cook. If she's anything like you, I'll bet she was a wonderful woman."

Heat crept over her like a shadow.

"So what's in her book?" he asked. "If you don't mind telling me?"

His genuine interest surprised her.

"Sweets, mostly," she said. "Apparently, she was quite a baker."

"*Ah,* pastries." A wicked grin spread over his face. "That means she was sweet."

Lindsay blew out a breath. "That's not a cliché at all, is it?"

Carlos chuckled. "What's wrong with that? People who bake tend to be kind and homey by nature—think grandmas. I, on the other hand, am a savory man. Not a sweet bone in my body."

"Well, you've got a point there. But I'm sure some big, burly pastry chef would just love to hear himself described as *sweet.*"

They laughed together.

"So you and I have losing our mothers in common."

Lindsay pursed her lips against the pang that inevitably pierced her heart when the subject of death came up. Even though she'd lost both of her parents, it didn't make it any easier to console others. Plus, was this off the record or part of the interview? It would be heartless to ask.

As if reading her discomfort, Carlos shrugged. "Not much love lost there. First, she abandoned me to my *abuela*'s care, then she went out and drank herself to death."

He said the words matter-of-factly. She grimaced. "I'm sorry."

He waved her off. "Nah. No need. What my mother lacked in affection, *Abuela* made up for tenfold."

"This is the grandmother who taught you to cook?"

He nodded, and a warm glow enveloped her at the thought of a little Carlos with his *abuela.*

"Were you an only child?" she asked.

"Yes."

"Me, too. Were you a lonely kid?" she asked, sensing that they just might have that in common, too.

He turned to her, looking very serious. But he didn't answer her. Their gaze linked, and the night suddenly seemed very quiet except for the faint roar of the sea. Only then did she realize how far they'd walked—all the way down the path that stretched from the city center down to the cliffs that bordered the beach—far enough to escape the hustle and jostle of the city to the natural roar of the water.

Funny, it didn't seem as though they'd walked that far. But they had, lost in each other's company, discovering that they had more in common than they might've imagined.

She crossed her arms, surrendering to a shiver that wasn't completely caused by the drop in temperature.

"Are you cold?" he asked. "Here, take my jacket." Before she could protest, he'd already draped it around her. It held the warmth of his body and smelled faintly of soap, leather and spice…and something indefinable that made her want to bury her nose in the collar and breathe in deeply.

He walked over to the waist-high retaining wall that bordered the sheer, rocky drop down to the water below.

"This is what I wanted to show you." He gestured for her to join him.

"The beach?"

Curious, she made her way over to stand beside him.

"Do you hear that?" he asked.

They stood silent for a moment, Lindsay straining to hear something, but just what, she wasn't sure. All she could discern was the sound of the wind and the waves slapping the rocks below.

"Earlier, you asked about the difference between South Beach and Cedar Inlet. It's similar to the contrast between downtown St. Michel and this." He made a sweeping gesture toward the sea. "Though South Beach might be a little rowdier and this beach a bit more extreme than Cedar Inlet. But at heart, the contrast is the same. I guess I've always connected better with nature than with people—well, most people. Let's just say there are certain types I prefer more than others."

They leaned on the wall, their shoulders a breath apart, not quite touching, but the vibrations radiating off each other were nearly palpable.

"If you're not a people person, then how the heck did you end up in the restaurant business?"

He shrugged. "Funny the path life sends us down, huh?"

The lilt of his accent set loose a swarm of butterflies swooping in Lindsay's stomach. Or maybe it was the nearness of him and the realization that they were alone—and the sudden rush of desire that trailed in the butterflies' wake.

"I *was* a lonely kid," he said. "The kind of lonely that can only be understood by someone who's felt it, too. You know, not belonging. I can't imagine that you were that kind of kid."

"Ah, but I was," she said. "Sometimes I still am."

"I don't believe it." His voice was a sexy whisper. "You can talk to anyone. You fit in anywhere. How is it that the lonely child in you overcame her affliction?"

She shrugged, aware of how he was looking at her. "It was difficult growing up under my father's roof. He was good to me—always made sure I had what I needed. But no matter what I did, it felt like I never quite measured up to his expectations. I suppose I was always trying to prove to him that I wasn't a failure. The only time I came close to making him proud was when I was reporting for WKMO. He took such pride in telling everyone that his daughter was on television every night. But then when I..."

She stopped, backpedaling away from the bad memory. She didn't want to get into it. Why ruin an otherwise good evening by drudging up parts of the past that couldn't be changed? *Her past.* They were supposed to be talking about him, for God's sake.

"You were saying?" he prodded.

"Let's just say one of the biggest disappointments of my father's life was when I lost that job."

He reached out and touched her arm.

"*Lost* the job?"

She held up her hand. "I don't want to talk about it."

"Fair enough," he said. "But look at you. You've come a long way since then. I think he'd be proud of who you are now."

Would he?

He smiled. In the clear moonlit night, she could see that the smile reached his eyes. Mmm, those incredible green eyes that looked darker than ever tonight.

"Funny thing is, sometimes I don't quite know who I am." The words escaped before she realized what she was saying. She should leave. Because her head was swimming and she was saying way too much. She was supposed to interview this man tomorrow. Supposed to be professional. She needed to have the upper hand, be the one in control. But he was looking at her mouth and she was leaning into him. When he took her chin in his big hand and drew her closer, she felt his warm, wine-scented breath so near that every feeling—every dream and desire she'd had since the first moment she'd set eyes on him that night at the castle—shimmered to the surface. Since then, all she'd thought about was the way his arms would feel around her, the way his lips would taste….

Then he kissed her. Despite the longing, the kiss surprised her. The tentative touch and softness of his lips were a sexy contrast to his masculinity. The warmth lingered, burning away the chill in the air. His mouth was so inviting and even though a voice of reason sounded in a distant fog in the back of her mind—she really shouldn't be doing this—she had to have one more taste.

He pulled her closer, enveloping her in that scent that threatened to drive her insane. Again, he dusted her lips with a featherlight kiss, then a playful nip. When his mouth finally covered hers, he kissed her with such an astonishing passion, it felt like it came from the soul.

The deep, demanding kiss had her reeling, as yearning pulsed through her body. And the way he touched her…one hand in her hair, holding her possessively in place, while the other slid down, caressing her back, edging its way underneath the hem of her blouse until the skin-on-skin contact made it exceedingly hard for her to catch her breath.

A low groan of desire broke through the sound of the elements, and she realized it had come from her. If she knew what was good for her she'd stop now….

Or…in a minute…. She just needed…one…more… taste—

Without warning, Carlos pulled away. Muttering something about it being late, needing to get back. The contrast was jarring, and she stood blinking, trying to regain her equilibrium. He'd gone from heated passion to cool business in the time it took to extinguish a flaming burner on a gas stove.

"What's wrong?" she asked.

"I just realized how late it is," Carlos said.

The excuse sounded ridiculous, even to himself. But how could he explain that he'd stopped kissing her because he never should've started in the first place? That he had no idea the taste of a woman could potentially drive him over the edge, making him want things he had no business wanting? Not right now.

He led her away from the wall, back on the path toward town. They walked in awkward silence.

Tonight, he'd been way out of line, asking her too many personal questions when he should've kept the focus on business. On tomorrow's interview.

Even more important, he should've never lost sight of his plan. A plan that didn't include a woman in his life. Even so, something at the most base level urged that not only did Lindsay have the potential to be part of the plan, but she could be the center of his world.

Donna had taught him a hard, expensive lesson about the cost of building his life around someone else. And because of that he'd promised himself it would never happen again. Of course, that didn't mean he'd become a monk. There'd been women since Donna. Several, in fact. And each one had been a beautiful distraction, but nothing more. Not a single one had cut to the core of him like Lindsay had, making him want things he hadn't thought about in a very long time.

Even if he went back on the promise he'd made to himself, with everything he'd planned for the next year, the timing was bad. It was the wrong time to start something. And even worse to start something he couldn't finish.

Hell, maybe it was even wrong to agree to the interview because it was crystal clear that when it came to Lindsay Bingham, he had very little control.

Somehow she'd managed to break through the barriers he'd erected. And tomorrow, they'd both go their separate ways. He was off to the Vienna Food Show, and she'd go wherever the *Diva* path led her next.

The chance of their paths crossing again was slim to none. Unless one of them compromised.

Compromise was too great a sacrifice to ask of either of them.

Chapter Five

It was just a kiss, Lindsay reminded herself as she walked the six blocks from the hotel to the festival grounds.

The thought made her head hurt almost as much as the bright St. Michel sun glaring on the white tents dotting the *Parc Fête* green. The morning was much warmer than the previous night. St. Michel weather was schizophrenic. Its warm days almost made a person forget it was early December.

Very much in the same way that Carlos Montigo made her forget herself last night.

She blinked away the thought as she neared the festival entrance. Despite yesterday's disarray, the workers had miraculously managed to pull everything together in time for the show. Too bad she hadn't been able to pull herself together rather than necking with Carlos Montigo like a hormone-ridden teenager.

"Bon jour," she said as she flashed her press credentials at the security guard posted at the entrance. He smiled appreciatively, muttered something in French, and motioned her through the gate.

"Merci. Au revoir," she said.

Even though hours had passed, she could still feel Carlos's kiss on her lips. She touched her mouth, but the sensation didn't go away.

In the bright light of day, she didn't know which hurt more—the wine-induced headache or her pride for his having kissed her and run.

Actually, it was her conscience that was giving her the most trouble.

She was such an idiot.

What was she thinking, jeopardizing her job by kissing the subject of her first interview?

Self-destructive idiot—as evidenced by the way her body reacted as she remembered Carlos Montigo's kiss.

She pressed her fingers to her lips, leaving a smudge of red lipstick on the tips.

After more than seven years away from the camera, not only did she have the pressure of filming her first segment in front of the boss, but now she'd compounded the difficulty by adding a headache and a dash of sexual tension.

She'd never been much of a drinker and she should've known better than to indulge in more than one glass of wine with dinner. But she and Carlos had talked so easily. And he kept pouring. All too soon she'd lost track of where one serving started and the next began.

Honestly, it was hard to tell which had been more intoxicating, the wine or the man.

Ha. Both were the cause of a massive headache.

Last night, he'd been so interested in her. Asking her questions. Absorbed in her answers. Drawing common parallels before he led her to that secluded, moonlit spot where he'd kissed her senseless.

Even thinking about it made butterflies flutter in her stomach.

Thank goodness, after today she wouldn't have to worry about being sucked in by Carlos Montigo's tractor beam. After today, she'd never have to see him again. It was a good thing, but for some ridiculous reason the thought left her feeling more empty than relieved.

Again, she held up her identification to security. This time she entered the press tent, happy to take shelter from the bright morning.

Since Sam had some preliminary camera work to take care of early this morning, Paula, Chandler and Lindsay had agreed to meet at the tent an hour before taping the show. Leaving her sunglasses on, she set her purse on a table and fished for more lipstick, some antacid and aspirin, swallowing the latter down with bottled water.

She was starting to feel better. Thank goodness the dry toast and weak tea, which she'd gotten from hotel room service, combined with fresh air and pharmaceuticals were already starting to make her feel human again—except for the uncomfortable memory of last night and the awkward mix of dread and anticipation of seeing Carlos again.

A mélange of food aromas filling the air didn't exactly help things. Ordinarily, Lindsay would've found the smells irresistible, but her stomach had churned itself into a nervous knot as she watched Chandler and Paula walk toward her.

"Lindsay, my love," Chandler greeted her with a kiss on each cheek. "You look beautiful this morning, darling. Are you excited?"

Okay. Well, so far so good. At least she didn't look like death warmed over.

"Paula wrote a wonderful script for you." He nudged her. "Give Lindsay a copy so she can study her lines."

Script? What script?

Paula set a pile of white poster boards on the table behind her and offered Lindsay a stack of smaller stapled white pages, but she didn't make eye contact as the paper changed hands.

"Since when do we use a script? Yesterday, you pointedly told Montigo we didn't work that way, that we wing it."

Paula acted like she didn't hear her.

"Well, today we do," Chandler said. "Things change all the time. While you were out wining and dining, Paula stayed up all night putting this together, and I must admit, I'm over the moon for it. It's brilliant. Exactly what I want. Smart. Edgy. Provocative. Just the direction I want to take the show."

Provocative? Edgy? Oh, God.

Lindsay flipped past a cover sheet to the first page and what she saw nearly made her choke: a total rehashing of the scandal.

It was a complete bait and switch from what they'd discussed with Carlos yesterday in his suite.

"I can't say this." She glanced up at Chandler, horrified. "I promised him we'd look forward, not back."

Paula, who was uncharacteristically quiet, looked impassive as she gazed at a spot somewhere over Lindsay's shoulder, still refusing to meet Lindsay's gaze.

Chandler frowned.

"You can't promise things like that, Lindsay. Especially when the mission of our show is to dig into *uncomfortable* territory."

He paused and the silence was deafening.

Oh, God. He was right.

She just hadn't expected her first assignment to be *this* uncomfortable. Under other circumstances, it wouldn't have been. Stupid mistake to let fleeting attraction cloud business.

"Why don't you give it a read through?" Chandler suggested. "Take it from the top."

Lindsay hesitated, and he rotated his hand in an impatient gesture that suggested she should get on with it because he was losing his patience.

Lindsay swallowed against the lump in her throat.

"*Er*...okay...*um*...I'm here with celebrity chef, Carlos Montigo." Lindsay knew her delivery was flat, but what did they expect on a cold read? She cleared her throat.

"He's staging a comeback with a new cookbook. But I'm getting ahead of myself. You remember the big debacle a couple of years ago, don't you? The refusal of the much-coveted Michelin star, which prompted the *Miami Herald* to dig into his background? The falsified résumé eventually cost him his job. Carlos, give us a little background. What possessed you to lie? How did you think you could get away with it? And most burning, who are you to turn up your nose at such an honor?"

There was a note written in the script, which Lindsay read aloud:

"At the end she should make a crack about it taking

a person with a huge ego to refuse a Michelin star…? Possibly tease that he should change his name to Carlos Mondo Ego."

What the—?

Now it was *her* turn to frown at Chandler and Paula.

Paula spoke for the first time. "I figured the crack would come more naturally if you worked it out on your own. But consider the Mondo Ego bit. It's funny."

"No, it's not."

Oh. My God. There was no way…. It was one thing to craft a report herself—in her own words—but it would be too difficult to regurgitate someone else's barbs.

Especially when she'd given her word to Carlos that she wouldn't delve into that territory.

And *Mondo Ego?*

All Lindsay could do was shake her head.

Chandler frowned so hard his brows nearly formed a single line across his forehead.

"Why are you shaking your head?" he asked.

"Seriously," Paula muttered. She rolled her eyes. Then, for the first time, her gaze locked with Lindsay's and the tiniest gleam of passive-aggressive self-satisfaction betrayed her motives.

She knew exactly what she was doing. She'd embarrassed herself by offering up the idea of the wine and goat man. When Chandler had reinforced how off the new track her segment idea was, Paula knew she had to redeem herself—and all the better to take a stab at Lindsay in the process.

Two birds. One stone.

Lindsay glanced at her watch. "We tape in less than an hour. I don't see how you can change plans the morning of the show and expect me to—" Lindsay fanned through the pages and shrugged. "I won't have this memorized before we tape."

Paula smirked. "I figured as much. That's why I made cue cards."

She turned and lifted the stack of poster board off the table. Sure enough, written in bold, black letters, each piece of poster board contained part of the script—verbatim.

"We need to practice before we start taping," Paula said. "Why don't we take it from the top again, and this time do a complete run-through."

We?

There was no "we" in this whatsoever.

"No," Lindsay said. "I need to work on this alone."

Paula sighed. It was the sound of someone at her wit's end.

"There's no time." Paula snapped her fingers. "Come on. Start at the beginning. Let's go."

Lindsay fought the anger spinning inside her.

She had to hold her breath for a moment until an eerie calm settled around her. But in the span of a few seconds her head cleared and she felt more in control.

"I am going to go over there." She pointed at an empty table on the other side of the tent. "I'm going to sit there *alone* and go over my lines. I don't need a coach. I don't want any feedback. I need to do this by myself."

Her voice was so low and steady that she almost didn't recognize it.

Paula opened her mouth to say something, but Chandler cut her off with a wave of his hand. "Leave her alone, Paula. She knows what she needs to do to prepare. Let her do it."

Lindsay mustered her best professional smile for

Chandler, nodded and walked away, knowing exactly what she had to do.

The only problem was, she had no idea how the heck she was going to do it.

The outdoor kitchen stage where Carlos would do the cooking demonstration was abuzz with last-minute preparation—food handlers were chopping and dicing; prop masters were moving and arranging; light and sound techs were testing and adjusting. People were rushing around, as busy as ants in a colony.

As the audience began to fill with early arrivals, Carlos waited backstage, out of the fray, sipping a triple espresso, trying to read the *New York Times*, trying not only to wake up, but to shore up his concentration. It was difficult with all the commotion—and everything that had transpired over the past twelve hours.

Maybe he should've stayed at the hotel until just before showtime. But he'd been antsy and needed to get out and clear his head so he could think. A lot of good it was doing him since all he could think about was seeing Lindsay before they came face-to-face with a television camera pointed at them.

Even the thought of the cameras made him a little anxious. *Maybe this wasn't such a good idea after all.* But just about the time he'd reached the edge of his mental ledge, he'd think of Lindsay and he'd back away from the edge.

If he'd known how he'd lose himself in the taste of her gorgeous mouth, would he have gone to dinner with her?

Probably.

He gazed up at the cloudless sky. It was so clear this

morning, that perfect robin's egg–blue that Mother Nature reserved solely for December. He wished he could borrow a bit of that clarity and put everything into perspective.

He'd awakened with the taste of Lindsay on his lips. Wrapped in a gauzy fog of half sleep, he'd craved more. He'd even reached for her, but all he'd found was the cool, unused pillow on the empty side of the king-size bed.

The bite of disappointment had jolted him fully awake, and he knew it was a good thing he hadn't found her in his bed. Not with the day they had ahead of them. Not only were they taping the segment, they'd be doing so in front of a live audience coming to see a cooking demonstration—the first live show he'd done since his life was turned upside down.

Even that didn't stop his body from responding to the thought of waking up with her naked and in his bed.

As he'd showered, shaved and prepared for the day, his mind kept drifting to the way she'd looked in the moonlight, to the moment his lips met hers. He couldn't stop thinking about the way she tasted, the way she felt in his arms.

Now here he was on the set, pondering at least one hundred reasons why kissing Lindsay Bingham had been a bad move. Reasons such as how he needed to focus; how he needed to reclaim some of the career ground he'd lost over the past two years; how getting involved with a woman right now was absolutely impossible—especially one like Lindsay Bingham who'd hit him like a drug.

He stretched his legs out in front of him and tilted his face into the sun, soaking in the warmth. His mind drifted to the way she'd looked last night with the moon shining on her blond hair; her eyes looked as dark as the sky.

A man carrying a table of props stumbled over Carlos's legs, nearly falling. But he caught himself in time.

"Sorry, man." The guy was American. "Didn't see you there."

"No problem. Are you okay?"

"Yeah, no harm done," the guy said.

Carlos scooted his chair back farther into the corner, between the backside of the stage and a stack of crates that jutted out, forming a half wall. Out of the line of traffic, he refolded his paper and tried to concentrate on the latest news in the United States.

Until he saw her.

Maybe he'd glimpsed her out of the corner of his eye. Maybe it was a sixth sense that alerted him to her presence. But there she was, with Chandler, Paula and Sam huddled around her.

Sam looked casual and Paula looking uptight and awkward as she shifted a bulky pile of what looked like white poster boards in her arms.

When she unloaded the stack on the table, Carlos saw that there was writing—bold, black letters that he couldn't quite make out.

Cue cards? Maybe if he could have a look at them he could get an idea of the questions Lindsay was going to ask him. Normally, he would've just been straightforward and asked. What was the harm?

But they were so adamant yesterday about not scripting the show. Well, it didn't take a rocket scientist to know that you had to have a script to have cue cards.

There must be a reason for the secrecy, and he

would've bet money that the crew would refuse to enlighten him before they started taping.

Well, even if he got a look at only the first couple of questions he'd have an idea of the tone of the interview.

He'd just have to wait until the right moment.

Just then, right on cue, Max rounded the corner and slapped Chandler on the back. Working it, just like a good PR flack should.

He laughed and talked with the *Diva* crew for a moment. Then he gestured toward the steps that led to the stage. They all followed him and disappeared through the curtain at the top, leaving the cue cards on the chair where Paula had deposited them.

He made his move quickly, picking up the cards and reading through each one.

"What the hell?"

It was an entire rehashing of the scandal. Exactly what Lindsay had promised him they wouldn't do.

His blood boiled.

The only mention of the new cookbook was a passing reference at the very end. But there'd be no time to talk about it. Not when her three-minute spot was spent raking the muck.

He was stupid for trusting her. Because all reporters were obviously cut from the same mold.

For a split second he considered simply refusing to do the interview. He didn't have to do it. He could do his cooking demonstration without *The Diva Dishes.* It was no skin off his nose.

But even though it would put Lindsay behind schedule taping her show, his refusal didn't seem like it would set her back much. After all, she had the entire Food and Wine Festival to draw from.

Well, as far as he was concerned, they'd sealed their deal with a kiss last night. While he was never one to kiss and tell, he intended to collect the endorsement he was due.

Chapter Six

"Cut!" Paula yelled, tapping the cue cards. "Why aren't you following the script?"

"Script?" Carlos frowned. "What script?"

"While we were out last night, Paula wrote a script," Lindsay whispered.

Carlos looked warily back and forth between Paula and Lindsay. "May I see it?"

"No!" Lindsay and Paula yelled at the same time.

At least they agreed on something.

Carlos shot her a knowing look, as if he sensed a conspiracy and wasn't a bit happy about it.

"What's going on here?" he whispered, exasperation weighing down his words.

"Nothing, just follow my lead," she whispered back.

Suspicion darkened his eyes. He even looked a little

disgusted, like he didn't trust her. With how this must look, she didn't blame him.

"Lindsay, would you please join us over here?" Chandler waved her over. Paula and Sam were already huddled around him.

"We're looking unprofessional," Chandler said as he frowned. "We need to get our act together. Pronto."

"If *she'd* just follow the script," Paula demanded, "we wouldn't have a problem."

Okay, this was war. Enough was enough. Lindsay had had her fill of Paula's attitude and she was tired of making excuses for the woman. Especially since Paula was making her look bad in front of Chandler on the day when she most needed to prove that he hadn't made a mistake by hiring her.

"You see, the thing is, the script stinks." Lindsay looked Paula square in the eyes and held her gaze for a beat before she turned to Chandler. "I won't do it. It's not…"

As she searched for the words she needed, she glanced at Carlos, who was staring a hole through them. It was obvious he could hear what they were saying. Why had they even bothered stepping away from him?

"It's not natural," Lindsay finally said. "I would never say the things Paula's written, and I don't see how you can justify springing a script on me one hour before we tape—even if you do have cue cards. You can't expect me to change course when I already had something in mind. You know, after last night—" She glanced at Carlos who smiled at her—kind of sarcastically. She looked away and lowered her voice. "After having dinner with Carlos. Talking to him. Interviewing him."

Kissing him.

Her cheeks flamed. Resisting the urge to press her

hands to her face, she hoped to God the blush wasn't obvious to the others.

Chandler scowled. Arms crossed over his chest, one hand stroked his chin in a contemplative manner. Lindsay couldn't tell if the gesture was positive or negative.

"Come on," Paula prodded. "The audience is getting restless out there."

"Yeah," the stage manager chimed in. "He needs to be on stage. Now."

"All right," said Chandler. "We can't hold them up. We need to get with the program or we'll miss our shot. At this stage in the game, Lindsay needs to do the interview the way that's most comfortable for her. You two need to get on the same page."

The look that flashed in Paula's eyes could've sparked a fire of global proportions, even though the evil eye was only directed at Lindsay. Not the boss, of course. Even though she was cloaked safely for now in Chandler's special dispensation—Lindsay knew there'd be hell to pay after this segment was complete.

Carlos watched as Chandler's huddle broke. Something didn't smell right.

"Sorry about that," Lindsay said. "Why don't we take it from the top?"

"Would you care to let me in on the secret?"

"Secret? There's no secret," she said. "Just a little confusion, but we're good now."

"Are we?"

She nodded, all business. There was no trace of the soft, vulnerable woman he'd held last night.

"I guess I'm a little confused over this phantom script, since you told me you didn't work with one."

"There is no script."

He quirked a brow. There was no way he'd let it go that easily.

"You told me Paula wrote a script."

"She did, but we're not following it."

"Why not?"

"It wasn't the direction I told you we'd go with this interview. And, I...I keep my promises."

If she hadn't thrown him a curveball before, she had now. "So, you and your producer are at odds? That doesn't exactly instill a sense of comfort."

"I guess you just have to trust me."

Yeah, right. There it was. That word.

"Why should I trust you? First you say there's no script, then we get to the set and—"

"Because I'd say at this point you don't have much of a choice, do you?"

"I don't have to do this interview."

Of course, he didn't mean it. But he wanted her to sweat for a moment. He was well aware that Chandler and his crew were listening. Where was Max? He could use a little backup right about now.

"Look, that's your prerogative. But backing out right now won't do either of us any good."

The woman didn't give up easily, and he found that devastatingly appealing. Even so, this was no time to let down his guard any more than he already had. He simply needed to get through the next few hours, and then he never had to see Lindsay Bingham again.

He ignored the strange way his insides constricted at the thought. That was the only way to get through this. The way it had to be. But in the meantime, it didn't mean he couldn't have a little fun reminding her of the deal they'd sealed with that moonlit kiss.

"I'm backstage at the St. Michel Food and Wine Festival with Carlos Montigo," Lindsay said to the camera.

She knew she'd be nervous, but she had no idea just how rusty she'd be. She felt clunky, as if the muscles in her face weighed tons. The camera light was impossibly bright. It was all she could do to keep from drawing a complete and total blank as she spoke, making herself look like a deer caught in headlights.

Maybe in the future a script would be a good idea—as long as she wrote it and didn't leave Paula to her own devices.

So Sam could get the shot in the tight confines of the backstage area, she and Carlos had to stand so close their arms pressed against each other. Hers were slightly in front of his and she couldn't tell if the heat she felt was nervous energy or if it came from him.

In a very strange way, this heat was her touchstone, the thing that kept her going.

"So, Carlos, you've done it again, you've written another cookbook, which you're releasing here at the festival. Can you tell us a little bit about it before you go out and cook for your fans?"

There was a flash of something in his eyes—something that resembled surprise, but she couldn't quite define it. It was there one instant and gone in a flash.

"Sure Lindsay, thanks for hanging out with me today." He moved his arm ever so slightly, leaning into her as he talked. "This cookbook means a lot to me, because it lets me get back to my roots."

Something brushed her back. It was so whisper soft,

that at first, she wondered if she might simply be imagining it. But then the pressure was unmistakable—it was Carlos's fingers stroking her bare back beneath the hem of her blouse, dipping just slightly below the waistband of her skirt.

Lindsay flinched. "What are you doing?"

His hand fell and he flashed a killer smile that could've charmed a nun out of her habit.

"I'm glad you asked." His hand was on her arm now. Yes, it was definitely the heat of him she'd felt before. "I'm heading out on stage, because they're telling me it's time for the cooking demonstration I'm doing here at the festival."

His gaze snared and held hers for a couple of beats more than was strictly professional, then, for a split second his eyes dropped to her lips. "I do hope you'll join me because I have lots of things to show you, Lindsay."

Then he winked.

And that was all it took to render her speechless. What the—?

"Carlos, what are doing?" she whispered.

"Come with me and I'll show you."

With that, he mounted the short flight of wooden steps that led to the stage, pausing at the top to turn and crook his index finger, beckoning her to follow.

He was messing with her. That's what he was doing.

Had he lost his mind? Touching her like that on camera—even though no one could see? But they could certainly see him leering at her like he was ravenous and she was prime rib.

If this was about the script—she glanced at Paula, who was standing with her hands on her hips, sporting a bemused expression that said loud and clear she was fully enjoying watching Lindsay flounder.

Out of the corner of her eye, Lindsay saw Chandler making a hand motion, indicating he wanted her to follow Carlos onto the stage.

Ugh…

For lack of a better idea—or a plausible reason to avoid walking into Carlos's fire—she did just that. With Sam in front of her, she ascended the steps that led to the stage.

It was make it or break it time. This was becoming her mantra. Holding on to the rickety metal handrail, she shored up her courage and decided, if Chef Boy Mondo Ego could dish it out, he'd darn well better be able to take it.

As soon Carlos saw her peering through the curtain that cordoned off the backstage entrance, he said to the audience, "There she is, ladies and gentlemen, *The Diva Dishes'* Lindsay Bingham."

The crowd broke into spontaneous applause.

"Didn't I tell you she was beautiful? Come out here, darling."

Darling?

As the audience applauded, she cringed inwardly, but resisted the urge to fidget, determined not to act as awkward as she felt.

She met Carlos center stage at the kitchen island and resolved that it was time to take control of the situation.

Her mind raced, discarding options such as secretly goosing him in the manner that he'd surreptitiously slipped his hand beneath the back of her blouse and trailed his fingers along her bare skin, or reverting back to Paula's script, calling him Carlos Mondo Ego. But she knew better than straying from the high road.

One had to be quick on her feet to play dirty pool in front of a live audience and not come off looking like a jerk. Since Lindsay was more the type to think of the perfect comeback fifteen minutes after the fact, sparring and digs weren't a luxury she could indulge in with the camera in her face.

"Well, this is quite an audience, Carlos," she said, instead. "Thanks for letting *The Diva Dishes* join you today."

"My pleasure," he said. "I've cooked up all kinds of surprises for you."

Surprises? There was that word again. His grin was a side dish of pure mischief.

"I'll bet you have." She smiled as she held his gaze. "You seem like the kind of guy who'd just be full of *surprises.* I'm going to keep my eye on you."

The audience unleashed a collective *ooh* that only seemed to egg him on.

"That would probably be a good idea, love."

More *oohs.*

"Oh, come on now," she said. "Don't encourage him."

They laughed.

Okay. That was good. A friendly crowd.

She felt her body loosen up.

"So, Carlos, your new cookbook, *Carlos in the Kitchen* is published by a house called Lone Wolf Press. *Hmm,* Lone Wolf? That's fitting, isn't it? Given your history as a guy who seems to enjoy being the only cook in the kitchen?"

"Lone Wolf is a small press, and I was honored to have them publish my book. Today, I'm preparing a recipe from *Carlos in the Kitchen.* Would you like to help me?"

"I'm not a chef, but I'd be happy to assist you."

"That's the point of this book," he said. "Actually, that's my philosophy as a chef. You don't have to be classically trained to prepare delicious meals."

"And you are self-taught, correct?"

He narrowed his eyes at her, as if he wasn't sure where she was going with this. He was probably bracing for her to dredge up the dirt that got him fired in the first place.

Good. It was nice to turn the tables on him—even if would only be for a moment.

He started it. What did he expect?

He picked up a knife and cut the end off an onion, then quirked a brow at her.

A challenge.

"We're roasting a chicken and vegetables today. A perfectly roasted chicken is easy and elegant, but at the same time, it's also the world's best comfort food. But before we begin, does everyone know how to chop an onion easily and safely?"

He was talking to the audience again, and they murmured their curiosity.

"Okay, let me show you," he said. "Lindsay, my love, would you please help me?"

He was baiting her, calling her *love* and *darling.* If she ignored it, maybe he'd stop.

"I don't know, Carlos. Onions have the same effect as tear gas on me. Will your method keep me from crying when I chop?"

"Only if you work fast, which this method will allow you to do. But until you master the technique, I suggest that you light a candle when you're chopping—the flame will burn away the sulfuric fumes, and that's what makes you cry."

"Really?"

"Well, that and cutting your fingers. So come over here and help me demonstrate the best way to hold my…*utensil*…"

Oh my God. He did not—

The audience *oohed* suggestively. Lindsay want to drop down and crawl into a cabinet. Instead, she kicked Carlos as hard as she could and still remain inconspicuous.

"People, people, people," Carlos tsked. "I don't know what your dirty minds are thinking, but Lindsay is a lady. Let's keep it clean. I want to show her how to hold a knife so that she keeps all her digits."

He took her hand and raised it to his lips the same way he had that night at the wedding. Only this time he nipped at her knuckle. She flinched. What the heck was he doing?

He handed her a large knife and moved a small cutting board with an onion on it in front of her.

"First, you need to hold the knife right." He slid her hand down and repositioned her grip so she held the handle where it met the blade. "This gives you more control."

Control was good. She'd certainly felt out of control since meeting Carlos Montigo.

"Curl the fingers of your left hand—the one holding the onion—under, and angle the top of the blade toward your left hand, so that the sharp edge goes away from your fingers that are holding the onion."

She squinted up at him, unsure of what he meant. That was the problem with letting her mind wander.

"Let me show you," he said.

He came up behind her and slid his arms around her, his right hand on her hand that was holding the knife, his left on top of her hand that was holding the onion.

As the audience whistled, egging him on, every nerve in Lindsay's body sang.

His arms around her made her feel strangely breathless, but if she stuck to her mental list of interview questions, she'd get through it.

Wouldn't she?

"Like this." He applied enough pressure to gently curl the fingers of her left hand back. He turned the knife in her right hand so that the blade angled away from the fingers holding the onion, so that the top of the blade grazed her fingers, but the sharp edge posed no danger.

"This technique has saved countless fingers." He said the words in her ear, even though he was talking to the audience. His breath whispered across her temple, sending shivers skittering up her arms.

"You see," he continued while holding her hand, guiding her as she chopped the onion. "With your fingers curled under and the blade angled away, you won't get yourself into trouble. Although, something tells me you like finding trouble."

More applause and whistles.

She found herself extremely conscious of him—his scent, clean, with a hint of spice; and his body, how it was pressed against hers, engulfing her as he invaded her space. She hated herself for it, but her body responded to the sheer virility of him.

Her head spun and she drew in a deep breath, inhaling a strong whiff of raw onion.

The ensuing burn was all it took to set the tears flowing.

Pulling out of his grasp, she swiped at her eyes. The onion-induced tears were starting to cloud her vision.

"See, I told you," she said.

He looked her over seductively and her heart turned over in response.

"Don't cry," he joked. "Here, let me help you with that. Was it something I said?"

He reached out and with the pad of his thumb, wiped a tear that had just spilled over her bottom lashes.

More *whoops* and cheers from the audience.

"It's just the onion." She swatted his hand away. "Umm…thanks, I've got this."

Carlos smiled, then picked up the cutting board with the remnants of the onion and set it on a counter behind them, out of camera range. In short order, a stagehand removed it.

He handed her a white dish towel.

"I'll bet you make all the girls cry," she said as she dabbed at the remaining tears.

"When I make a girl cry I always kiss the hurt and make it better," he said with a sly grin.

Again, the audience cheered. "Kiss her and make it better," someone called.

A rush of heat started at her neckline and spread upward. She racked her brain for a segue back to the cooking demonstration, but before she could open her mouth, Carlos had swept her into his arms as if she were weightless. She gasped as he dipped her back in a fashion that would've made a tango master proud.

She was putty in his arms. He bent over her, his lips a breath away from hers, and the audience went wild. She could feel his uneven breathing and her heart hammered foolishly.

The audience cheered and chanted, "Kiss her! Kiss her! Kiss her!"

But he didn't.

Thank God, because if he had, she probably would've melted into a puddle right there in the middle of the stage—she wasn't sure if it would've been from embarrassment or desire or because the world seemed to whirl around her in this upside-down predicament. She caught a glimpse of Chandler frowning from the side of the stage.

Oh, God. She'd blown it.

Utterly.

Completely.

Then, just as fast as Carlos had swept her into his arms, he righted her and started saying something about putting the onion in the chicken cavity after he slipped some herbed butter under the bird's skin.

Lindsay stood there blinking, wondering why the heck she hadn't stuck to the script.

Chapter Seven

"Why didn't you stick to the script?" Paula demanded once they were in the car headed back to the hotel. Lindsay had considered walking back alone rather than getting into a confined space with Paula and Sam, but somehow walking back to the hotel alone would've seemed like a walk of shame.

No, it was better to leave as a team and hold her head high.

"I thought the spot was *hot,*" Sam said.

Both women looked at him—Paula glared, Lindsay tried to figure out whether he was being facetious.

The spot was a disaster. She was sure Paula was secretly celebrating, reveling in the chance to skewer Lindsay with a chorus of passive-aggressive I-told-you-so's.

"Well, it *was* hot," Sam persisted. "The audience thought so, too."

Good old Sam. After working with him for less than a week, Lindsay liked him. He was the team's optimist—at least they had one. Casual and laid-back, Sam seemed to find the good in everyone and go wherever the wind blew him—or wherever *Bossy* led him.

Paula might be able to get away with leading Sam around by the nose, but she had another think coming if she thought she could push Lindsay around. A heart-to-heart was long overdue, and Lindsay knew it needed to happen sooner rather than later. Maybe tonight after the production meeting Chandler had scheduled to discuss the future production schedule.

Lindsay stared out the window and watched picturesque St. Michel roll by. Of course, that was *if* there'd still be a meeting later—since Chandler had left before they'd finished taping.

Her insides constricted at the thought. But before she could fall down the slippery spiral of self-doubt, Lindsay steeled herself, determined not to read anything into his leaving—because it wouldn't do any good. It would only drive her crazy.

She needed to borrow some of Sam's optimism.

Even if Lindsay had felt awkward, the audience *had* responded well. And Chandler hadn't stopped the taping. He certainly would've been within his rights to do so, if he'd thought the content was totally unsalvageable.

Unless he was just being courteous to Carlos, not interrupting the flow of his live show.

Oh, God.

Her head spun and she wiped her clammy palms on her skirt.

Stop it!

She could go back and forth all day, but he'd certainly tell her his thoughts in no uncertain terms at the meeting. Right now, it would only drive her crazy to ponder the what-ifs.

She just wanted to get past this debacle and move on. That's why she'd bolted before Carlos had finished his show. They'd finished taping, but he still had an autograph session to attend. It was Lindsay's perfect escape. She took it.

She didn't have to face him after the way he'd made a fool out of her in front of all those people. What hurt the most was how he'd made a mockery—albeit a private joke—out of what had happened between them the night before.

The jerk. If he'd been upset by the script, couldn't he tell she wasn't following it? After all, he was the one leading the show.

Next time she'd be the one in control.

"A complete and utter disaster," Paula muttered, and it was all Lindsay could do to hold her temper.

"I'm sure there's at least three minutes of footage we can—*use* for the spot." She'd almost said *salvage* but she'd caught herself just in time. She wasn't going to give Paula the satisfaction of knowing she was sick about the segment. "And just so we're clear, Paula. In the future, I'll write my own scripts."

She'd intended to keep the issues between her and Paula. To hash it out in private, not in front of Sam—or the driver. But suddenly this seemed as good a time as any. Especially since Paula couldn't seem to leave it alone.

"If there is a next time." Paula smiled. She looked absolutely evil.

Lindsay whipped her head around to look the woman dead in the eyes. "Excuse me?"

Paula smirked. "You just don't get it, do you?"

The car pulled up in front of the hotel.

"I certainly don't understand *you.* You've had a problem with me since day one, and I think it's time you and I got to the bottom of it. Let's go somewhere and talk about this."

But before Paula could respond, Lindsay's cell rang. Chandler's name flashed on the LCD screen.

"Hello?" She hoped to God her voice didn't shake.

"Lindsay, it's Carson. Please come up to my suite. We need to talk."

Carlos walked into the living area of the suite he and Max shared. Max was sitting on the couch, leafing through some papers.

He looked up and saw Carlos. "How'd the signing go? Sorry I had to bolt, but I had some business to take care of."

Carlos shrugged. "I sold about fifty books. Which, on paper, sounds impressive, but since there were upwards of two hundred people in the audience, I don't know if it's anything to get excited about."

"That means a quarter of the audience went home with a book. I have a feeling the other hundred and fifty will soon be clamoring for a signed copy."

Carlos shot him a questioning look.

"I just made some coffee," Max said. "You might want to pour yourself a good strong cup and sit down. We have something important to talk about."

At first, Carlos thought Max might give him hell about crossing the line with Lindsay, a don't-mess-with-the-one-who-gives-you-free-publicity speech.

He served himself a cup of Italian roast, and he began

formulating his defense. The show was over and done with. He'd just have to take his hand-slapping like a big boy and move on.

"Look, after today I'll never see her again," he said, taking a seat across from Max. "We left things on good terms and I think the segment was terrific."

Liar.

Lindsay left without as much as a farewell. He had come on a little strong today, but he'd trusted her. And she'd broken her promise.

She'd obviously done what she needed to do to get the story she wanted. In turn, he did what he needed to do.

All's fair...

"My philosophy is," Carlos said, "sweet talk them so they say sweet things about me."

Max looked confused. "What are you talking about?"

Carlos shrugged and sipped his coffee. He didn't have to explain himself. Besides, it was a moot point. It was over. He'd never look back except to ride the momentum the *Diva* spot would give him.

Max shook his head. He seemed to do that a lot these days, but that was part of the reason they got along so well. Max knew when to shut up and give Carlos room. Knew when not to push. Knew when to change the subject.

"So, I was talking to Carson Chandler. He, uh, has a business proposition for us. *Er*—for *you.*"

Carlos wrapped both hands around the coffee cup, enjoying the soothing warmth.

"What kind of business proposition?"

The guy was into all kinds of industry. Maybe he published cookbooks? If he wanted to pick up *Carlos in the Kitchen,* they could talk. Hell, if the offer was good enough just about anything was possible.

"He just bought the Epicurean Traveler Network and wants to expand this three-minute *Diva Dishes* infomercial for Chandler Guides into a full-fledged, hour-long show."

Max paused and fixed Carlos with a knowing look. Carlos wasn't quite sure what this had to do with him—except that maybe the spot would be an hour rather than three minutes. Did they have enough footage? Because if they needed more they'd have to follow him to Madrid for his next scheduled appearance.

In an instant, images of rediscovering his hometown with Lindsay on his arm and in his bed flashed through his mind. There would be no script. Just instinct and spontaneity.

Weren't they at their best together when things were spontaneous?

Nice daydream. But it would never happen.

"I'm sure you're aware Epicurean Traveler is a direct competitor of Food TV," Max said.

The mention of the Food TV bastards zapped the rush Carlos had been feeling and landed him in a bad mood.

"Right, and he needed your approval for this latest scheme? He's not trying to hire you away from me, is he?"

"Possibly, but it would be a package deal since he wants a male host to join Lindsay Bingham on the new show."

Another knowing look. This time with a broad smile.

"Montigo, he's considering *you* for the spot. He loved the chemistry between you and Lindsay. Said that was exactly the type of fire he wants for the show. This could be the answer to our prayers."

Carlos's mouth went dry as Max's words sank in. An unsettling bittersweet feeling loomed, setting off a war of conflicting emotions. On one hand this would be an opportunity to see Lindsay every day. On the other hand…he would see Lindsay every day.

Not to mention getting caught up in the grind of a network series again. He frowned at the thought of being owned by a television network—something he'd sworn he'd never endure again.

"I don't know, man," Carlos said. "It was such a mess last time."

"Chandler's astute. He's coming into this knowing damn well who you are, and more important, who you *aren't.* He doesn't care what happened before. If anything he'll parlay that into good PR for the show."

"No. No way." Carlos held up his hand as if he could repel the repugnant idea.

"But don't get ahead of yourself," Max soothed. "We have some negotiating to do."

Max held up the file. "This is the contract. We need to go over it. Chandler wants to meet face-to-face this afternoon."

For a long moment neither of them said a word. The silence was heavy. But finally, as if he couldn't contain himself any longer, a broad smile overtook Max's face.

"You're back, my man."

Max let out a whoop.

"Now look who's getting ahead of himself." Carlos took a long draw of his coffee, wishing the hot liquid could either infuse him with the same certainty and enthusiasm that had gripped Max—or at least wash away the longing to see Lindsay that was building inside him.

"It's my job to be optimistic about you. It's also my job to advise you. We're going to ask for better money—twice what he's offering."

"Twice? Wait a minute."

"If we ask for twice, we'll get a better deal."

Carlos set his mug on the glass-topped coffee table and then rested his elbows on his knees, pressing his hands to his eyes.

"I don't know, Max."

"What do you mean, you don't know? Most people would kill for a second chance like this."

Carlos was all about second chances. That was exactly the principle behind the restaurant he wanted to open. Giving kids who'd screwed up a second chance at life—a chance to learn a trade so that they could do an honest day's work and sleep at night with pride that they were making it on their own.

"I know that, but you know television isn't exactly the direction I wanted to go. I don't know if I have it in me to run that rat race again."

Max sobered. "It's either the rat race for the short run or you'll be on the road for God knows how long hawking your self-published cookbook out of the trunk of your car."

Though Max hadn't come right out and said it, there was an undertone that suggested if Carlos refused this offer, he'd be working out of the trunk by himself. Who could blame Max? He'd stuck with Carlos through the worst and here was their opportunity to dig themselves out.

The reality hit him like a strong punch to the gut.

Carlos leaned his head back on the sofa cushion and closed his eyes, trying to erase the image of Lindsay that kept running through his mind.

If this was going to work—if they were going to work together—they had to come at this platonically. The last time he'd let business become personal it nearly destroyed him and his career. But now he was stronger than that.

"Let's roll up our sleeves and hammer this out," Carlos said.

Chapter Eight

Lindsay stopped by her room to touch up her face before going up to Chandler's suite. On the phone, his voice had held his own particular brand of Carson Chandler urgency that suggested she get there sooner rather than later, but if he was going to chew her out—or worse—she wanted to go in with the confidence of knowing she wasn't a shiny mess.

Now, standing outside his door, she knocked straightaway rather than pausing to collect herself, because if she had, she might not have knocked at all.

"Come in," he called. "It's open."

When she reached for the door, she realized her hand was shaking. She took a deep breath, checked her posture and mustered her most confident smile before walking in.

"Hello." At least her voice sounded steady.

Chandler held up a hand, and she saw that he was sitting in a chair by the window, talking on the phone.

Oh. Oops.

"Can you be here by two-thirty?" he said.

She glanced at the grandfather clock. It was just after two o'clock now. Who was he talking to, she wondered idly as she looked around the suite, taking it all in—the antique furniture, the realistic Impressionist replicas, the marble-topped bar with its fine crystal stemware and Cognac decanter, the fresh flowers in the porcelain vase on the mirrored buffet.

In all her years she'd never been around such finery. Her father had always provided for her and done the best he could, but luxuries like this weren't part of their world. If he could see her now, he'd be happy that she was finally "doing something" with her life.

How many times had they fought about that?

A stinging lump formed in her throat.

If she thought about her father too hard, she'd get emotional. Right now she needed to stay positive and strong.

If Chandler was unhappy with her performance, she'd convince him she'd do better next time.

She *couldn't* lose this job.

"I know it's earlier than what we'd discussed." There was an edge to Chandler's voice. "I would really appreciate it if you could move it up in your schedule."

Suddenly, for the first time in a long time, a sense of purpose rooted inside her. She knew this job was something to fight for. She couldn't just stand by and let it slip through her fingers.

She'd approached this job tentatively, almost expecting it to end. Because didn't everything good eventually play out? Like Cinderella finally making it to the ball only to have everything she'd worked so hard for evaporate at midnight?

Maybe it was time she wrote Cinderella a new happy ending. For a nanosecond her thoughts skittered to Carlos and his kiss, his arms around her today.

This chapter of her Cinderella story wouldn't necessarily include a prince—at least not Carlos. Because right now, the story was about her.

If this job turned into a pumpkin, she'd have nothing. Not even her old Social Services job.

"Sorry about that, Lindsay." Chandler's voice startled her. She hadn't heard him hang up. "I had to take that call. Come over here and sit down. Tell me, how do you think today went?"

She studied his expression as she made her way toward him, but it was unreadable, which rattled her nerves again.

"Today was...interesting. It was a little...*unpredictable,* but I suppose that stands to reason since it was my first shoot in seven years. The important question is what *you* thought."

Her stomach churned.

Chandler frowned.

When he didn't say anything, fear knotted inside her.

Ooh. Oh, no.

She braced herself, waiting for the fallout.

Then a wide smile overtook Chandler's face. "I thought today was remarkable. *Perfect.*"

She had to purse her lips to keep the elation from escaping.

Then, slowly, she relaxed. For the first time since she'd awakened this morning, she was able to draw in a full breath.

"Thank you," she uttered.

"I must admit," he said. "After getting off to such a rough start, I was a bit skeptical at first. But as soon as the two of you got going, the chemistry between you and Carlos Montigo was mind-blowing. I came back and looked at the raw footage and I loved it."

Chemistry?

Mind-blowing?

Was it that obvious?

She bit her bottom lip at the memory of Carlos's kiss. She willed herself not to blush. Miraculously, somehow she was able to maintain her composure.

Everything was going to be okay. No, it would be more than okay. She still had a job, and from that moment she vowed to do everything in her power to make sure each show going forward was the best she could deliver. She would write her own scripts. She'd remain perfectly professional and not cross the line with the subjects of her interviews. She'd—

"Which brings me to something else I wanted to discuss with you." Elbows on the arms of the chair, Chandler steepled his fingers. "Do you remember me expressing my wish to expand *The Diva Dishes* into a full-length show?"

The bottom of Lindsay's stomach fell, causing her to inhale sharply.

"Yes."

Was this going where she thought it was? Ooh. She shouldn't get her hopes up. She nodded, trying to act casual. Not like she was about to jump out of her skin.

"Since purchasing the Epicurean Traveler Network, I've been in a position to expand the show. The only thing holding me back was finding the right hosts."

Hosts? As in plural?

"Today, that search came to an end."

The pause was almost as tantalizing as the prelude to a first kiss. The silence lingered, hovered, like lips destined to meet. Almost...but not quite...yet. The vision of Carlos with his fingers laced in her hair, his mouth a whisper's distance from hers...the chemistry...the—

"I believe I have found that dynamic duo in you and Carlos Montigo."

She bit her bottom lip. Those were the words she'd anticipated. The offer she'd hoped for finally presented itself.

And with *Carlos?*

A warm glow flowed through her.

"Of course, the potential change was written into your contract," he said, "but there is an escape clause if need be. So tell me, is this something you'd be interested in?"

Her heart sang with delight.

"Absolutely."

Chandler nodded his approval. "Very good."

"Is Carlos already on board?" If it was the pair of them he wanted—a package deal—it certainly sounded like it.

"I made the offer to his agent earlier today. In fact, that was him on the phone when you arrived. We have some minor details to iron out, but I can safely say, yes. He is on board."

Her stomach performed an odd little somersault.

"When I first saw you," he said, "I had a hunch you'd be perfect. I simply wasn't one hundred percent sure if you were the woman for the full-length episode, because much of that hinged on finding the right cohost. You and Montigo absolutely cemented that today. Of course there will be a pay increase commensurate to the expanded camera time. My dear, I'll say this as a friend—you really should have an agent. So...?"

Her head spun. Chandler must have sensed as much because he spread the new contract out on the coffee table and pointed out the pay increase and the terms: four episodes to be filmed over the span of a month, one episode per week. Contract terms would either be renewed or terminated upon completion of the fourth episode.

Her body vibrated with new life.

She really did need an agent—or a lawyer. Someone to guide her through this. But reality was overshadowed by another feeling that kept bubbling up—the impossible joy of getting to see Carlos.

Every day.

She hadn't realized what an effect he'd had on her until now.

Of course, they'd have to set some things straight. Keep things platonic. There was no other way this would work. She'd nearly lost her head today. She hated being out of control like that.

There was a lot at stake, but she could handle it. The secret was to start thinking of Carlos Montigo strictly as a business associate.

From this moment on, that would be the extent of their relationship.

As the old grandfather clock struck two-thirty, there was a knock on the door.

"Ah, right on time. Come in," Chandler called.

Carlos and Max walked in, followed by a room service attendant pushing a cart heaped with a bottle of champagne in a sterling wine bucket, four crystal flutes and a mountain of strawberries surrounding a bowl of luscious-looking chocolate sauce.

* * *

She looked like a ray of sunshine, Carlos thought, as he gazed at her from across the room.

Their eyes locked and he sensed her stiffening. Her brown eyes grew a shade darker even though she smiled. For all outward appearances, she appeared happy to see him. He was probably the only one who sensed the whisper of a strain in her expression as she looked away, turning her attention to Chandler, who had leaned in to say something in her ear.

It wasn't exactly jealously, but there was definitely a proprietary tug as he spied Chandler's arm around her waist. It was a ridiculous reaction. He had no claim on her, especially if they were to work together for the next month.

Then in a flash, Chandler was walking toward them, welcoming Max and him, with handshakes and jovial slaps on the back.

"How wonderful to have my new cast together for the first time," Chandler said. "This calls for a toast."

The room service attendant popped the cork and poured the Dom Perignon into the glasses, handing each one to Chandler, who, in turn, passed them out.

"To the newest show on the Epicurean Traveler Network, *The Diva Drives.*"

They raised their glasses. As they sipped the bubbly, he snared Lindsay's gaze again, causing a tingling in the pit of his stomach. This time she looked away, with an odd twinge of disappointment.

"Diva Drives," Chandler repeated. "That will be the name of the show. Please have a seat and I'll tell you about the premise."

"Well, here we are," Carlos said as he settled next to her on the sofa.

"How about that," she answered, sounding almost glib.

The way the morning had turned out, he couldn't blame her. He supposed he'd have to explain his actions at some point. To clear the air so that they could work together.

Platonically.

But how ironic that if he hadn't set out to push her buttons, if she'd just come in and done the traditional interview about a new cookbook, perhaps they wouldn't be here now.

Not that it was all his doing. It was their—how did Chandler put it?—*chemistry* that sealed the deal.

The question was how were they supposed to maintain that chemistry and keep things platonic?

It would be like holding a lit match to a gas tanker—explosive.

Chandler sniffed his champagne, held it up to the light and regarded it for a moment before he sipped it.

"I had this vision of the two of you in a car driving through Europe," he said. "Hence the name, *The Diva Drives.*

"Of course, you'll get out and visit notable locals, interview interesting people, dine at fabulous restaurants. But the premise revolves around the chemistry of the two of you in the car. It will be as much about the journey as the destination."

Wasn't that the truth.

Chandler leveled Lindsay and Carlos with a knowing look. "Judging from the chemistry, if I didn't know better, I'd swear that the two of you were involved. But we all know how mixing business and pleasure can get tricky."

"No!" Lindsay said. "We're not."

Chandler flashed a patronizing smile. "I see the way

he looks at you." He turned to Carlos. "And I see you looking back."

"It was part of the show," Lindsay said.

"No, I'm talking about when the camera's not even on you."

So it began. You signed a contract and they took it for granted that they own you. Carlos waited for Chandler to throw down the gauntlet and prohibit personal involvement. There'd been nothing in the contract, so there was no way he could control their personal lives.

He slanted a glance at Lindsay, who stared straight ahead, her body language betraying nothing, despite the defiant set of her jaw and the slight upward tilt of her chin.

He couldn't blame her. It was insulting.

Then again, it was only for a month. For the money Max had managed to negotiate for him—enough to give his Cedar Inlet restaurant a healthy start—he could play by Chandler's rules in the short-term. Then he could take the money and run—whether they offered a new contract or not. And if this was anything like his experience on *Piece of Me,* he wouldn't want to sign on for an endless tenure of being owned.

He tried to ignore the voice inside that asked *what about Lindsay?*

"I'd like to take the footage we shot today, add to it and expand it into our first hour-long show. This works so well. We hadn't yet invested anything in a new intro for the new *Diva Dishes*—that was on the schedule for tomorrow. So we can fold in today's footage and we haven't lost anything."

"When did you want to start?" Carlos asked.

"Tonight," Chandler said as if it were a given.

Tonight. The guy didn't waste time.

Thinking of the appearances he had lined up for the next month, Carlos looked at Max, who seemed to read his mind.

"We have a slight problem," Max said. "Carlos is booked at various festivals around Europe. It could get costly if we back out at the last minute."

Chandler waved away the concern as if it were merely a pesky gnat. "E-mail my assistant a list and she'll take care of it. We'll pay any cancellation penalties incurred. I want to get this show on the road right away. Literally."

Chandler chuckled at his own joke and chased the humor with another sip of champagne.

So this was really going to happen, Carlos thought, as he glanced at Lindsay, who'd been unusually quiet. Probably for the best that they jump right in, because if he had a chance to think about it too hard, he might remember exactly what he was getting himself into—again—and run in the other direction.

"What about the production?" Max asked. "This is a much larger scale than *The Diva Dishes.*"

Chandler nodded. "Very good question. We will increase the crew, of course. Something of this scale requires at least four cameras and upwards of a ten-person production team. The good folks at Epicurean Traveler are gathering the crew, probably as we speak. The larger scale of this show is one aspect that makes it so exciting."

"Will you keep Paula and Sam?" Lindsay asked.

Chandler tilted his head to the side and considered her question. "I hadn't really given it much thought. But now that you mention it...hmm. One thing will be paramount is that we all work well together as a team. We will be pulling exceptionally long days. There won't be time for artistic clashes if we're going to shoot an episode a week. Lindsay, I realize there's been a personality clash between you and Paula. If you'd rather not work with her, I have no problem letting her go."

Chapter Nine

Lindsay wasn't avoiding talking to Carlos about what had happened between them earlier that day. Really, she wasn't.

The only reason she left the meeting so fast was because she had to talk to Paula.

She and Carlos would talk. Eventually. There was no avoiding it.

First, she had to talk to Paula.

It felt weird holding the fate of someone's livelihood in the palm of her hand.

That was essentially the way Chandler had left it. He'd gotten a call and had ended the meeting as quickly as he'd called it. He'd asked Lindsay to decide within the hour whether Paula and Sam stayed or went.

They had no idea how tenuous their jobs were. Chandler hadn't yet broken the news about the new show to them because he wanted to wait until Lindsay and Carlos were locked into place to avoid potential media leaks.

Apparently, Sam and Paula had been afterthoughts. It bothered her that Chandler could consider them so expendable. Maybe it was because she was in a there-but-for-the-grace-of-God-go-I state of mind, because hadn't she been fearing for her job when she walked into Chandler's suite?

As fate would have it, she happened to be on Chandler's sunny side at the moment. But she'd been in the fragile position of being superfluous before and the memory still haunted her. She wouldn't wish it on anyone.

Sam was a given. Of course he'd stay. He was talented and easy to work with. Plus, he'd been her ally from day one. Loyalty was important, especially in this business.

Still, despite all the friction with Paula, Lindsay couldn't in good conscious save Sam's job and kick Paula to the curb.

Maybe she was an idiot for giving Paula the benefit of the doubt. But since the woman had been with *The Diva Dishes* from day one, Lindsay wanted to give Paula a chance to save herself. She wasn't going to make the woman grovel, just simply explain why she had such a problem with Lindsay.

Maybe she was naive, but Lindsay clung to the belief that people were inherently good. If someone acted like a jackass, there was usually a reason. Not that it excused bad behavior, but in a gesture of goodwill Lindsay wanted to give Paula the chance to explain herself and to clear the air.

What Paula chose to do with that opportunity was up to her. It was a good sign that the woman had agreed to meet Lindsay for a cup of coffee. She hadn't pulled a sorry-I'm-busy, we'll-schedule-it-when-it's-convenient-for-me excuse. She'd agreed straight off, which made Lindsay believe that Paula really did want to work things out. To be fair, Lindsay had decided to be up-front with her right out of the starting gate.

The mood was tense as they placed their orders, but as soon as the server stepped away from their table, Lindsay said, "Thank you for agreeing to talk to me. I really want to get to the bottom of the friction between us."

Paula crossed her arms. A defensive gesture.

"I have to admit, part of me was curious to see if you still had a job," Paula said.

Okay. That wasn't exactly the tone she was hoping for.

The woman definitely knew how to push Lindsay's buttons.

"Look, I'm going to be frank with you. I still have a job. It's yours that's in question."

The look of utter astonishment on Paula's face was equal parts heartbreaking and vindicating.

"Mr. Chandler called the earlier meeting to tell me about some changes to the show. Some very exciting changes, I might add. My place is secure, but since the new format will require a solid team, he left it up to me as to whether you'd stay on with us. He told me to consider whether I could work with you, Paula. I have to be honest, at this point it's looking doubtful."

Paula opened her mouth to say something, but all that came out was a tiny sound, something like a cough.

"I'm not trying to be mean or rub your nose in it. I just want to know why you have such a problem with me."

Paula grunted and screwed up her face.

Strike two. *Come on, Paula. You're about to strike out.*

officials so that they could film the two of them driving up to the gates.

"Are *you* okay?" he said.

Someone had to break the ice since they were going to be working in such close confines.

She nodded.

He ran his hand over the dashboard. It was a lean machine and when Carlos first got a look at it, he was nearly dizzy at the thought that he'd be driving it for the next month. Only now that he was actually sitting in the driver's seat with Lindsay beside him, he felt a little subdued.

Whatever had initially passed between them had vanished. This cool, remote woman beside him wasn't the woman who'd inspired him to lose control. Because that's what had happened yesterday during the cooking demonstration. Even if he'd started out with the intention of teaching her a lesson about baiting and switching, somewhere between the feel of his hands on the bare skin of her back and dipping her into the almost-kiss, he'd lost control. He'd wanted to kiss her. Now, he desperately wanted to tell her so.

But all he could do was ask whether she was okay.

That was such a farce.

He wasn't okay and obviously she wasn't, either. So he resorted to generalities.

"Look," she said in a small voice. "I guess at this point it's best to just be straightforward."

He looked at her, trying unsuccessfully to see her eyes through the dark lenses of her sunglasses.

"I don't want to play games," she continued. "I don't understand what you were trying to prove yesterday. Acting like that...on the set."

He started to explain, or at least offer a reason, but she held up her hand and stopped him.

"I don't need explanations. I want your word that it won't happen again. We're on the same team now. We have to work together for this show to fly. So, truce?"

He reached out and pushed her glasses on top of her head.

"I need to see your eyes," he said.

She raised her chin defiantly, but her eyes belied her hard stance, suggesting that this was just as hard for her as it was for him.

"Truce," he agreed, gripping the steering wheel rather than giving in to the urge to run his finger down her jawline. "I think I mentioned at dinner the other night that I didn't enjoy working in television during my last show."

She angled her body toward him. "Actually, you didn't mention it. You were pretty tight-lipped about the past that night. Why do you bring it up now?"

She met his gaze.

Why *was* he telling her this now?

"Because as you said, we're on the same team now. Yesterday, you were the media trying to report the story you needed to report."

She started to protest, but he held up a finger.

"When I was in television before, I was burned very badly by the media and others I trusted. My actions toward you—right or wrong—were reflexive. I think we've both learned a lesson about not trusting. So as you said, truce."

She nodded in agreement.

"Just so you know, I didn't go back on my word to you. The story they wanted me to report wasn't my story. They had no idea I'd promised you we wouldn't look back—"

"I didn't know that then, but I do now. So let's leave that in the past."

They sat in silence for a moment, watching a tall, dark-haired man greet Paula and three production assistants. Comprised of sixteen members, the new crew was decidedly larger than the former *Diva* operation. It included four camera operators—of which Sam was the team leader—two audio technicians, and a ten-person production team. Chandler had kept Paula on, but he hadn't put her in charge of production. Strangely enough, the woman didn't seem to mind. In fact, she'd mellowed out, was actually trying to work as a team player.

"Is that Henri Lejardin?" Lindsay asked.

Her voice had lost its edge. She sounded more like herself.

Carlos shaded his eyes from the early-morning sun. Sure enough, it was St. Michel's minister of Art and Culture. As he'd promised at the wedding, Lejardin had dropped by the signing. Then after the new deal was signed and sealed with Chandler, Max had called him and arranged for the show to shoot some footage in and around the palace. Lejardin and Paula were walking toward the car.

As Lindsay and Carlos got out of the car to greet Henri Lejardin, Lindsay was once again overwhelmed with awe that this grand palace was now her good friend Sophie's home, and the country's handsome Minister of Arts and Culture was Sophie's brother-in-law.

Still, even that wasn't nearly as baffling as realizing that the man she'd been sitting next to in the car was turning out to be more real than she'd ever imagined. He'd actually cared enough to clear the air—to drag the issue out into the open and leave it there until they were both satisfied with the resolution.

Usually she was the one doing the repair work.

This was a refreshing change.

She found his openness devastatingly sexy, much to her dismay. If she knew what was good for her she'd check all sexy thoughts at the door. The pain of the sexual harassment complaint she lodged against her former boss still plagued her. Because of it, she'd lost her fiancé and her job. Even though that was in the past, the bottom line was Chandler had made it perfectly clear that he didn't approve of romantic fraternizing. Her head knew that was plenty enough reason to shelve any romantic notions of Carlos Montigo.

Now, if she could only convince her heart as much.

"Mademoiselle, so nice to see you again," Henri Lejardin said as he planted a kiss on each of Lindsay's cheeks. "Much has changed for you since the wedding. I must congratulate you on your success."

Henri was a tall, striking man. His perfect English was embroidered with enough of a French accent to add to his charm. His dark good looks hinted at a slight resemblance to his brother, Luc, Sophie's new husband, but Henri was not quite as intense as his older sibling. He was less reserved, and there was a hint of flirtation in his smiling eyes. Or perhaps it was just that certain brand of magnetic charm that was organic in wealthy, good-looking men in lofty positions. Where Luc could be compared to a French James Bond, Henri was more like Hugh Jackman with a French twist—a sexy turn that had nothing to do with the hairstyle, of course.

"Thank you, Henri," she said. "Have you met my co-host, Carlos Montigo?"

"Yes, we met at the wedding and then again at his cookbook release party at the festival."

The two men shook hands.

"Very nice to see you again," Carlos said. "I can't tell you how much we appreciate your allowing us to shoot at the palace on such short notice."

Henri's eyes twinkled as he flashed a blinding grin at Lindsay. "How could we refuse someone with such excellent references? Besides, her beauty makes us look good."

The compliment made Lindsay smile. "I'll bet he says that to all the girls." She turned to look at Carlos and—

Oh—

The way he was looking at her…

She was accustomed to men's appreciation—to looks of lust even—but Carlos's eyes held something altogether different. It was almost heartbreaking because they couldn't explore it as long as they worked together.

Chapter Ten

Working with the footage they'd already shot during Carlos's cooking demonstration, it only took three days to shoot the rest of the first episode in and around St. Michel. After that, they spent a week in Cannes shooting the second spot. Now they were in Toulouse, France, for the third *Diva* installment.

This morning, Carlos waited alone in the French Provincial dining room of the Leblanc Inn, the quaint bed-and-breakfast that had become the temporary Toulouse headquarters for the cast and crew. He popped the last bite of fresh-baked baguette—which he'd slathered with butter and homemade apricot preserves—into his mouth, and washed it down with a swallow of good, strong black coffee.

Men had waged wars for less, he thought as he heaved a silent sigh of satisfaction. The least they could do in this episode was pay homage to the delicious breads baked by Babette Leblanc, the proprietor of the Leblanc Inn.

He'd suggest it as soon everyone gathered for the daily production meeting. Right now, the dining room was empty. The dozen small tables, topped with lace cloths, waited unmussed for the *Diva Drives* barrage, which, according to his calculations, should hit any moment. Collectively, the group ran like a well-oiled machine adhering to plans and schedules.

It was amazing how seamlessly everything had fallen into place for the new show format. Here they were, already taping the third installment—three-quarters of the way through the contracted commitment. What a change from his experience on *Piece of Me,* which felt like an uphill battle from the get-go.

There was only one area that felt a bit shaky...his off-camera relationship with Lindsay. Since that first day in the car, she'd remained distant when they were alone.

Cordial.

Professional.

Platonic.

Actually, now that he thought about it, they never really had that much time alone. Whenever it was just the two of them, she'd find one reason or another to excuse herself.

When they were in a group, she was herself—smart, funny and open. What he liked about her was that somehow she always managed to cut through the crap and get right to the heart of the matter. But when they were alone, she'd close up tight as a clam. Her distance was her protection. He understood that because the two of them weren't so dissimilar in that department. They both could put on a good front when it mattered, but the armor was always at least part of the way up.

As if on cue, Lindsay entered the dining room. Chandler and Max were with her. All three offered Carlos hearty greetings.

Carrying herself with self-assured grace, Lindsay looked gorgeous. Her pale pink sweater brought out the rose in her cheeks and hugged her curves in a way that a man couldn't help himself but to do a double take. Paired with trim black slacks, the sweater looked so soft it begged to be touched. At the thought, blood surged from his fingertips to his toes.

Carlos fisted his hands into his napkin and cleared his throat. "Good morning."

"I'm glad you're here, Montigo," Chandler said over his shoulder. "We're on a tight shooting schedule today. All week for that matter. In fact, they're bringing Bella around in fifteen minutes."

Bella was what the cast and crew had affectionately named the red Ferrari.

As Chandler, Max and Lindsay helped themselves to coffee from the silver server on the buffet, Babette Leblanc entered the room with a tray of steaming brioche. She offered Lindsay first choice, and Lindsay plucked one out of the basket and held the warm bread up to her nose, savoring the aroma.

"Ah, *merci.*" She sighed. "This is heaven. Right here in my hands. And if I keep eating this way, Carson, I won't be able to fit into the car and you'll have to fire me."

"But what a way to go," Max said as he placed his saucer of coffee on Carlos's table and helped himself to two brioches.

"Carson," Lindsay said, "we need to work a segment

on Babette." Lindsay gestured to the woman, then to the room. "This place and her fabulous bread."

Great minds.

Chandler considered the suggestion. "That might make a nice starting point for the segment. We could open here and close at the winery in Bergerac. Talk to Paula about it."

Lindsay nodded and started to set her breakfast down at the small table next to Carlos, but hesitated when Chandler pulled out a chair next to Max.

As Carlos motioned her over, their gazes locked. It was the first time she'd looked at him in the past ten days. Since they'd been working together, she'd looked past him. Through him. At everything but him. But now she was finally looking at him. In that split second, in which time seemed to grind to a screeching halt, her eyes spoke volumes. And what they said hinted at plenty of unfinished business.

"Lindsay, join us over here," Chandler said.

As she tore her gaze away, Carlos wondered if the tension was as obvious to Chandler, because to Carlos, it felt as palpable as the thick home-churned butter on the table.

Lindsay set her plate down and Carlos stood and pulled out a chair for her. The gesture seemed to startle her, but she recovered fast.

"Thank you." Her voice was light—almost unnaturally so. But what did he expect with the boss sitting between them?

Then the rest of the crew began to stream into the dining room, and Chandler asked them to serve themselves coffee and whatever they wanted to eat. "But be quick about it because I have a full agenda to discuss and you must be on the road to our first location within the half-hour. No time to waste or we won't get everything done."

In short order, everyone gathered around.

Chandler brushed the crumbs from his navy blue fisherman's sweater and called the meeting to order.

"I appreciate how hard everyone's working during this holiday season. That's why I feel a little guilty leaving you all today to go back to New York, but I'm thrilled with the St. Michel and Cannes episodes we've shot and in my absence, I have all the confidence that you will continue the good work you've been doing. I must have one more meeting with the executives at the television station to tie up some loose scheduling ends. Then I will head home to spend Christmas with my family. If I don't, my wife will never let me hear the end of it."

A round of obligatory laughter rippled through the room as several people nodded their understanding of his predicament.

He went over the schedule.

"Christmas is five days from today," he continued. "That's one reason I'm rushing to get this shoot wrapped up, so that you all can spend Christmas with your families."

Carlos blinked at the realization. Despite the near freezing temperatures and homey holiday decorations strung up around the inn, Christmas had snuck up on him.

Further south, St. Michel and Cannes had offered balmy days and pleasant evenings. Besides, they'd been so busy it hadn't dawned on Carlos that it was Christmas week.

Since his divorce he hadn't enjoyed the holidays. Not that Max wasn't good company. But it would be nice, for a change, to kiss someone under the mistletoe and hold her tight at the stroke of midnight as they ushered in a new year.

Reflexively he glanced at Lindsay, who sipped her coffee and listened as Chandler detailed the schedule and what they needed to accomplish so they could have the week off. They'd be trekking through a cheese cellar in Roquefort, France, and then tomorrow, they'd pack up camp and head three hours northwest to Bergerac, home of some of the most incredible French vineyards and wineries.

After that, they were free until after the new year, when they'd reconvene in Paris.

Paula cracked a good-natured joke about how she was *finally* getting her wine and cheese segment, which encouraged more laughter. The woman had done a serious attitude about-face.

He might as well work through Christmas, Carlos thought as he listened to everyone making merry after learning of Chandler's gift of a week off.

How was he going to spend the holidays?

The thought of ringing in the new year alone rang hollow.

It was the smell of him that undid her, Lindsay thought as the two of them sat in Bella. It was all she could do to resist the urge to lean in and bury her nose in that place where his neck met his shoulder, the way she had that night at the beach, and breathe in that intoxicating mix of soap and leather that was so distinctly Carlos.

It had taken an extraordinary amount of willpower to resist.

Iron willpower.

But she'd managed.

That's why she'd insisted on driving the majority of the time. In the driver's seat, she could keep her eyes on the road and her hands on the steering wheel.

So, on the occasion when they were confined to the close quarters of Bella, the seat belt, steering wheel and ribbon of highway before her were her safety net.

Or chastity belt, of sorts.

Maybe that was a little extreme, but they hadn't slept together. Thank God. And this arrangement was meant to keep it that way.

Remarkably, Carlos had been amenable to her being in the driver's seat. Most men, she mused, would've demanded at least equal time putting a car like Bella through her paces.

That's why it caught Lindsay off guard when Chandler had insisted that they mix it up a bit today, that Carlos should drive in this episode. Of course, Lindsay was smart enough to know that a person who valued her job wouldn't argue with the likes of Carson Chandler. Nope, she'd hand over the keys and strap herself in for a long, bumpy ride.

Figuratively speaking, of course.

They were taping the journey from the inn to the cheese cellar today. On the way to meet the *affineur*, it felt a little awkward not being able to drive. Of course, they wore mics and had cameras in their faces, which left little time for personal small talk.

They still weren't working from a formal script, but one of Paula's jobs was to come up with specific talking points she constructed from the lightning-fast research she did on each area they featured on the show. The talking points were designed to keep the conversation natural and flowing. Relevant.

Even armed with those talking points, she felt as awkward as a teenager on a first date—unsure where to look or what to do with her hands.

So she kept her hands in her lap and looked straight ahead out the window. She never looked directly at the camera, except for an intimate aside in response to one of Carlos's particularly flirty or suggestive remarks.

Never directly at Carlos, if she could help it.

But she couldn't always help it.

As they drove to the cheese cellar, Carlos followed close behind a flatbed truck with a camera mounted to it for the tracking shots.

Toulouse was a beautiful city with a spicy blend of cosmopolitan and history. Lindsay had read that some of the city's old mansions dated back to the Renaissance. Filled with gardens and squares, it was an exciting commingling of past and present, preservation with accents of modernity.

Carlos and Lindsay wore small earpieces that fit inside the ear with wires that wardrobe had tucked away down collars and underneath scarves, so that the apparatus was invisible to the camera, but Carlos and Lindsay could still hear cues from the director, David Crawford.

"Okay, everyone, listen up," David said. "We're about ready to approach the area where I want to film the drive-by. Start with the first talking point, Carlos, in three…two…one…go—"

"So, Lindsay, you're finally giving me a turn behind the wheel. You're not one of those women who always has to *drive,* are you?"

Slanting a glance at her, he chuckled, playing it up for the camera.

She feigned offense.

"What, are you suggesting I'm controlling, Carlos?"

He shot the camera a do-I-even-have-to-answer-that look.

"But Carlos, sweetheart, I'd never dream of trying to control you, oh, unmanageable one."

He tore his gaze from the road to give her a smoldering reaction. That made it suddenly very hard to breathe. But it was all for the camera, she reminded herself.

In turn, she shot the camera a look of her own, which inspired Sam to give them a thumbs-up.

"Cut!" David called. "That was great. Perfect. You smoked it."

"We smoked it." Carlos held up a fist for Lindsay to bump. She did. He kept his eyes on the road and it gave her a chance to look at him.

On the way to the cheese cellar, they skirted Carcassonne, a walled medieval city that rose like a mighty dragon in the distance. Since they were on such a tight schedule, Lindsay and Carlos didn't stop to tour it—a small crew would film what they needed and the editor would splice together audio and video of they city with footage of Carlos and Lindsay in the car.

On cue, Lindsay said, "Oh, look at that. It's as if we've time-traveled to a medieval storybook city."

"Carcassonne dates all the way back to the twelfth century," Carlos answered. "It's one of Europe's best-preserved walled cities, complete with turreted towers—fifty-two, to be exact—and Gothic architecture. It's perched high on a prominent headland that overlooks the vineyards of the Languedoc region. Even from down here, the view is extraordinary."

"It really does look like a picture from a book of fairy tales. I wish we could go inside."

He smiled. "Princess, I should've known you'd fall in love with Carcassonne. But sorry, if we stop, we'll miss our appointments with the cheese maker and the vintner. Maybe next time?"

Lindsay sighed. It wasn't all affect for the camera. Even though she'd spent a month in the St. Michel palace, Carcassonne called to her.

Maybe next time.

"That was perfect, you two," David said into their ear pieces. "Let's do the short intro to the cheese caves and then you two can hang out until we get to the cheese man. Sound good?"

They agreed and without much ceremony went right to their talking points.

"So, Lindsay, did you know that the Languedoc area, where we are now, isn't one of France's best know gastronomical regions?"

"Really?"

"Yeah, it's sort of had a tumultuous history—at one period, the southern region of France spoke an entirely different language from the rest of the country, called Occitan."

"Is it still spoken today?"

Carlos shook his head. "Not by many people, but this area still remains sort of an anomaly because of its geographical placement."

He paused, loving the intensity with which she listened to him.

"Think about it," he continued. "They get great seafood from the Mediterranean, which borders the southeast coast. To the west, the Pyrenees, where we're going, offers not only great cheese, but wild fowl. To the east, they have the vibrant gardens of Provence, and to the southwest is Catalonia and its Spanish influence." He reached out and touched her arm. A benign gesture. Nothing inappropriate, certainly not sexual. Yet, her whole being filled with wanting.

"No wonder the Languedoc region is gastronomically confused."

Yeah, but not as confused as she was.

Since the planes of Languedoc were largely dominated by vines, Carlos and Lindsay had to head for the town of Roquefort in the Midi-Pyrénées, into sheep and goat country, to find the famed cheese caves that were home to the famous blue cheese.

When they arrived, Carlos was surprised to find the subject of their interview, cheese maker Girard Martin decked out in a red shirt, suspenders and a Santa hat. The slight, petite man was not much older than he was, early forties at the most. The getup, which Paula had to ask him to modify so that the spot could be timeless, gave him an elfin appearance.

Though Carlos might have been taken aback by Monsieur Martin's clownish appearance, he wasn't at all surprised by the way the man took an obvious shining to Lindsay.

As they walked the short distance to the caves, Martin offered Lindsay his arm—a gesture David liked—and fussed over her, making sure she watched her step, protectively steadying her at times. Carlos thought Girard's European disregard for personal space was excessive.

Obviously, he'd been away from Europe long enough to become accustomed to the American standard of keeping one's hands to oneself. Not that watching another man put his hands on Lindsay bothered him. It was simply that he knew how much she hated anyone making a fuss over her.

As they walked Girard droned on. And on. And on. "I was born in the beautiful town of Toulouse. You are staying there, yes?" He didn't pause long enough to let them answer. "I lived there until I was sixteen. Then I left to come here to work as an apprentice. In my early years, I never imagined I would become an *affineur,* that the cheese caves would be my destiny."

Caveman. The guy was a virtual Neanderthal the way he was pawing Lindsay.

"Ah, here we are," he said.

As they reached the entrance to the cave, Girard slid his hand up Lindsay's shoulder, kneaded it a couple of times, then slid his hand down her arm on his way to open the door. When he turned away, Lindsay took a step back and shot Carlos a look that said loud and clear she was a little bothered by Martin's attentiveness.

The moment he opened the door, the smell slammed into them like a wave of dirty socks. Or maybe it was baby spit-up. This was particularly ripe.

Girard inhaled a hearty breath through his nose, flaring his nostrils and closing his eyes. "Ah, smell that? Isn't it beautiful?"

As a chef, Carlos was used to various odors—delicious and foul—particularly after working in restaurant kitchens most of his life. Most smells—like the pungent cheese or the onions that had made Lindsay cry—didn't bother him. But not everyone had that sort of immunity to smells.

Martin droned on about himself and how the phenomenal cheeses he produced would be ordered by some of the top chefs in the world and would make their way into some of the world's best restaurants.

Carlos arched his brows at Lindsay, and she made a face at him, then smiled. Sam was right there to catch it all on camera.

Right. The camera.

This was good stuff for the show. Good chemistry—playing off each other's strengths and differences. Their dissimilarities amounted to combustible on-screen presence. They were good together that way. Their strengths and differences seemed to bring out the best in the other…on the job. And, of course, he'd already had a taste of how those ebbs and flows complemented each other when no one was watching.

As Sam jockied his way around Martin to get into position to film their exploration of the cave, Carlos noticed Lindsay looked a little green. Her eyes were wide and her mouth was pressed into a thin line. Obviously, she was doing her best to be a good sport, but she wasn't enjoying this.

Carlos turned his back to the camera and mouthed, *Are you okay?*

Her eyes flashed, but then she steeled herself.

Fine, she mouthed back.

By this time, Girard had produced a flashlight from inside the cave. With it, he motioned Carlos and Lindsay inside.

"Come in. Come in," Girard said. "Just shield your head should a bat decide to fly at you."

"Bats?" Lindsay stiffened. "There are bats in here?" She started backing up.

Martin threw his head back and laughed. "No, silly girl." He grabbed her hand and yanked her forward. "There are no bats in here. I am making fun with you."

Carlos smiled to himself. *Bet she loves that. Way to endear yourself.*

"Ah, Girard," Lindsay said. "You're just a funny guy, aren't you?" In the narrow cave entrance, Lindsay did a little sidestep around Carlos so that he was between her and Girard. As she brushed past him, she shot Carlos another conspiring look. This one wasn't for the camera.

It was just for him.

For the first time in a long while, they were connecting on more of a personal level.

Hmm...maybe ol' Girard wasn't so bad after all.

As they made their way into the cave, the Frenchman droned on. "My love of cheese began when I was a teenager. I was fortunate to meet people who would guide me to understand how the magnificent flavors and aromas of fine cheese enrich the senses."

Carlos glanced back and saw Lindsay rubbing her nose. Girard and Sam moved deeper into the cave. Lindsay moved up closer behind Carlos.

"Magnificent aromas?" she whispered in his ear. "That's debatable."

Sam and Girard moved ahead, taking the light source with them, leaving Carlos and Lindsay in the dark. Her voice washed over him in waves of ecstasy. Her sweet, hot breath in his ear warmed him from the inside out, tempting him to turn so that they'd be face-to-face, their lips a whisper a part.

She put her hand on his back, but they didn't move to catch up with the others. What the sound of her voice had started, her touch promised to finish.

Not a good idea, his head warned. Oh, but his body begged to differ. Awareness pumped through him, making him hyper conscious of the smell of her—honey and nectar with hints of something he couldn't quite define. He wanted to press his lips to hers and taste her and try to figure out the mystery ingredient.

"I hope he was right about this place being bat-free," she whispered again.

Before he could think better of it, he reached back and grabbed her hand so that her arm snaked around to the front of his waist. She didn't recoil, simply stood there, her curves flush against his back.

What had started between them that first night was still alive and well, pulsing between them, refusing to be ignored. The fact that she didn't pull away was proof that things weren't finished. And he intended to continue what they started—Carson Chandler and *The Diva Drives* be dammed.

"*Yoo-hoo!* Where are you?" Girard Martin's accented voice filled the air. "Did we lose you?"

Carlos gave her arm one last squeeze, pulling her in closer one last time—for now, Lindsay Bingham.

For now.

As they made their way deeper into the cellar, catching up with the others, Lindsay said, "So, Girard, who was the first brave soul to pick up one of these smelly hunks and decide to taste it?"

Frowning, Martin stared down his aquiline nose at her. "Smelly hunk?" He looked insulted. "I have no idea. However, once *I* was introduced to the world of cheese, my life was forever changed. *Pour moi,* life is a never-ending journey *du fromage* and no matter how many varieties are laid in front of me, my insatiable appetite shall never be satisfied."

"Yeah, I'll bet," Lindsay murmured.

Chapter Eleven

It was too dark to film on the drive back to the Leblanc Inn. So the production crew decided to call it a day. Carlos and Lindsay headed back in Bella.

It was a strange day. Strange flipping back and forth between the on-camera chemistry and the safe-distance platonic friendship, because suddenly keeping it platonic felt more like acting than the on-screen relationship.

Now that the sun was setting, it was hard to know how to act, what she should say to him about today in the cave or if she should say anything at all. But suddenly all she could think of was what it would feel like to be in his arms, kissing him, touching him. And that was much too dangerous.

She could still keep her distance behind this wall she'd erected. Staying cocooned away from him would only hurt a little, but if she let herself get in any deeper, there'd be too much at stake. Her job. Her heart.

"Quite a day, huh?" Carlos said.

Lindsay nodded. "I can't believe I was right here in Carcassonne and didn't get a chance to check out the upper city. I'll have to come back. Someday."

There was a beat of silence.

"Let's go there," he finally said. "Let's go now. We could go for dinner and a look-see."

"Are you serious?" Lindsay blinked. "No, Carlos. It's an hour outside of Toulouse—"

"It's only five-thirty. We'll be there before seven." He glanced at her. "That's plenty of time for a nice dinner and a walk."

Her mind skittered back to the last time they had a nice dinner and a walk. "I don't know if that's a good idea, Carlos."

"Why not?"

"You know *why not.*"

He looked at her blankly. "No, I'm afraid I don't. Is it me? Do you not want to have dinner with me?"

"No, it's not you…."

"Because if it's me, just say so, and I'll leave you alone. But something tells me that's not what you want."

She didn't say anything for a moment. She couldn't find her voice. Or at least the voice of reason that would say the right thing—the sensible thing. Something like, *No, I don't want your lips on mine, your hands on my body. I don't want you around me and certainly not in me….* The problem was, she wanted all those things.

He eased the car off the deserted road onto the gravel shoulder, and sat there for a moment with the engine idling, his hands clutching the steering wheel. They were in the middle of nowhere. No houses, no shops, only the rolling French countryside, over which the sun was setting and turning the field vivid shades of amber, orange and violet.

"The thing I hated most about working in television," he turned and looked her in the eyes, "was that sometimes it felt a bit like selling my soul to the devil. Suddenly they owned me. I was their puppet who danced when they said dance and sat quietly in a corner until they wanted me to perform. Only I didn't sit quietly. I caused way too much trouble, so they cut me loose."

"You sound so cynical."

"Maybe I am." He shrugged. "I almost turned down this job."

"But you didn't. How come?"

He laid his head back on the headrest and grinned at her. "Ever the inquisitive reporter, aren't you?"

She squirmed a little. *No.* She was so bad at it.

"I'll make a deal with you," she said. "Level with me and tell me your side of the story about why you lied about your credentials and I'll have dinner with you in Carcassonne."

He made a face, and blew out a forced breath between his lips. *Pfft.* And his dismissal of the question might have worked, except that she'd caught the look that flashed in his eyes before the wall went up.

"I lied. What more is there to say?"

"I don't believe you."

He laughed, but it was anything but humorous. "So you're saying I'm lying about lying?"

"Not exactly. I think there's more to the story than what you're telling me."

"And what if there is?"

She wanted to ask him how she was supposed to trust him if he wouldn't be straight with her.

"Carlos, I am not the enemy. We're on the same team now, remember? Why won't you trust me?"

"Why should I?"

What? Oh, for God's sake—

"Fine. Never mind. Let's go back to the inn."

Lindsay turned her head and stared out the window as she waited for him to ease the car back onto the road.

"I hadn't intended for everything to get so out of hand," he said.

Lindsay turned and looked at him.

"My ex, Donna, had huge social aspirations and worked hard to make the restaurant the hot spot in Miami, while I cooked. She did a good job, actually. Through her connections, I got guest judging spots on a few reality TV shows and eventually I landed *Piece of Me.* The only thing wrong was that Donna had padded my credentials. By the time it mattered, she'd already put these false claims out there and it was awkward to retract them. So against my better judgment, I let it ride because I never dreamed anyone would bother to research my background. God, I was stupid. I knew it was wrong, but once it got to the point where people were paying attention, it was too late to retract it. What was I supposed to do? Post a big sign that said, *I was too busy cooking to notice that my wife fabricated my résumé. I don't have a Grand Diplome from Le Cordon Bleu and I never worked at the Élysée Palace in Paris?*

"I was an idiot to let her do it. So I can't blame anyone but myself for the mistake. I knew that, and before I signed the contract with Food TV, I leveled with them. I told them the truth and how the false résumé came to be—and actually that was strike one against my marriage. Donna didn't want me to confess, but that's beside the point. When I laid it all out on the table with the network execs, I did it verbally. I didn't ask them to sign anything acknowledging the disclosure, because they said, 'Le Cordon Bleu and the Élysée Palace sound a lot sexier than saying you're self-taught. Let's just leave it as is.'"

He shook his head.

"I took them at their word. God, I was such a naive bastard. And of course, when the house of cards came tumbling down, they pretended to be just as surprised as everyone else. They wanted to distance themselves. So they suddenly had no recollection of that meeting."

Lindsay reached out and touched his arm. "I'm really sorry."

He pulled away. "Don't feel sorry for me. I was an idiot. The last thing I want or deserve is pity."

She shook her head. "Don't be ridiculous. I don't pity you. It's just not right."

For a moment, no one said anything.

"So, the paper started digging when you refused the Michelin rating, right?"

He nodded, a faraway look in his eyes.

"Yep. They took great pleasure in finding me out because originally they set out to prove that I'd refused the stars because I was trying to be different or difficult or I thought I was too good or some equally inane reason that had nothing to do with the real reason I turned down the honor."

Lindsay paused, hoping he'd tell her why. But he didn't. Not immediately.

"So why did you turn it down?"

"I was scared to death. That's why."

He looked away and she wanted to reach out and hold him.

"The television show had kept me away from Prima Bella Donna so much, I felt so out of touch. Because the kitchen, the food, that was my touchstone. That's why I left all the front-of-the-house business to Donna. She was good at schmoozing. I was good at cooking. They offered the award based on my kitchen, well, not entirely, but the quality of the food is a large part of it. But being away from the restaurant, I had no control over what was happening in the kitchen and the pressure to keep the rating was just too much and while I'm spilling my guts, refusing the rating was strike two against my marriage—Donna had a fit. But I held firm. Honestly, I never wanted to be *that* kind of chef in the first place. I sort of got caught up in the whirlwind of it all—and all this fame and fortune pleased my wife. My *ex-wife.* To her, the fame was great and the money was even better…but it was so far from who I wanted to be… God, I hate sounding like the victim. I hate sitting here and saying this all *happened* to me. I sold out. I should've had the balls to put my foot down before it spiraled out of control."

He shook his head as if he could erase the thought.

"Well, isn't that what you were doing when you refused the Michelin rating? It seems like it was the start of taking back control of your life."

He snorted. "It was the beginning of the end. Food TV suits fell all over themselves trying to disassociate themselves from me and they terminated my contract for falsification of credentials. Of course, it was my word against theirs. They lied and said no such meeting took place where I told them about the padded résumé."

Memories of her own failed attempt to take on the big boys crashed down.

"So, the long and short of it is that Donna filed for divorce and got her beloved Prima Bella Donna and the house. I didn't care. I just wanted to get the hell out of Miami. That's when I moved to Cedar Inlet."

He shook his head. "So there you have it. The undoing of Carlos Montigo. Happy now?"

Happy? "Well, no. Why would that make me happy?"

"That's why I don't like to talk about it. Why I didn't tell my side of the story, as you put it, to the press. The only thing it would change is it would amplify the fact that I was a jackass for not being more in control of my own life."

The way he was looking at her nearly broke her heart. She reached out and put a hand on his arm because she didn't know what to say or what else she could do.

"So, are you ready to explore Carcassonne?" he asked.

Chapter Twelve

With its cobblestone streets and medieval buildings all decked out for the holidays, the upper city of Carcassonne was indeed like something from a fairy tale.

Carlos half expected to spy Father Christmas and his team of reindeer flying through the inky sky. What he wouldn't give right now for Santa Claus to grant him a do over in the spirit of the holidays.

He hadn't intended to spill his guts and tell her the entire pathetic story. Beyond Max and Donna, who was long gone, no one knew the entire story. Not even the television bigwigs who'd cut him loose.

He felt exposed.

Lindsay must think him a moron for letting his life spin so far out of his own hands. Of course, she didn't act that way. In fact, she seemed more open now than she had in a long time.

As they roamed the walled city, he did his best to shake it off. It was his problem, and he needed to get over it. Or at least not let it spoil the evening.

Before they headed to Carcassonne, they called Paula to let her know they were making the stop. Lindsay had been uncomfortable with simply disappearing with the car—"It's a Ferrari, for God's sake. I think we'd better check in."

She was right. It was better to report in than to have them send out a search party. But checking in went against his grain.

They wandered the streets, peering in shop windows, *oohing* and *aahing* over the quaintness of the unique little city and its festive holiday mood. It had turned colder outside now that the sun had set. Though the high temperature had only reached the low fifties, Carlos was willing to bet it was dipping down into the forties.

Lindsay turned up the collar on her coat and rubbed her gloved hands together. He had the sudden urge to take her in his arms and warm her with his own body heat. Heat that was increasing as he thought of how it would feel to hold her again—and this time do it right.

When they turned from Rue Saint Louis onto Place Auguste-Pierre Pont, Carlos spied an elegant-looking restaurant called La Barbacane.

"How about this?" he suggested. "I'm in the mood for some good authentic food and I'll bet this place can serve it up."

It also happened to be the only restaurant in Carcassonne with a Michelin rating. One star. Just like the one he'd refused.

Maybe he was a glutton for punishment, but he

wanted to try it. To see how La Barbacane compared with Prima Bella Donna.

"It looks wonderful," said Lindsay.

He held the door open for her and they stepped into a wonderland of stained glass and rich paneled walls. A petite brunette greeted them, smiling warmly as they approached.

"Deux pour le dîner, s'il vous plait," Carlos said.

"I have a very romantic table by the window over looking the rampart," she said.

They checked their coats and followed her to their table.

It really was a magnificent view of the gardens, the Citadel ramparts, with a glimpse of Carcassonne in the distance. But the menu, which was based on seasonal ingredients, looked even better. It boasted such mouth-watering offerings as green ravioli with *seiche,* a species of octopus, in a sauce of its own ink; crisp-fried cod with black olives; saltwater crayfish with strips of Bayonne ham. Simply from reading the descriptions, he could virtually taste the flavors. His mouth watered and his heart ached a little as he realized how much he missed being in the kitchen.

Lindsay ordered the Breton lobster with artichoke hearts and caviar. Carlos had the organic free-range guinea fowl rubbed with vanilla and stuffed with truffles.

It was heaven on a plate, but the food was nothing compared to the way Lindsay looked.

His gaze was riveted on her lips, and all he could think about was how she would taste. In the wake of all that he'd unloaded today, kissing her was probably not a good idea. Yet there was something about the way her eyes danced in the candlelight and the way she was smiling at him. Something sensual that hinted at possibilities and desire.

Something that whispered a promise of what was to come before the night was over. Suddenly good sense seemed highly overrated.

The confession that left him feeling raw and vulnerable obviously hadn't changed her mind about him. If anything, he felt closer to her.

He shifted forward and lightly stroked her hand with his fingers. It was just a light touch, meant to give her the opportunity to pull back if she wanted.

But she didn't.

Instead, she gently took his hand, turned it over, palm down, and studied it. "When was your divorce final?"

"Why?"

"Your ring finger doesn't show any signs of a wedding ring." She traced the place on his ring finger where a wedding band would've gone. Then shook her head and released his hand. "You're always so defensive."

It was true, he reflected as the busboy cleared the plates. Since losing the restaurant and his marriage, he'd always thought it was an emotion he couldn't help—aftershock of sorts.

The waiter offered them dessert. Lindsay declined, saying the lobster was delicious and rich, but she had no room for another bite.

Looking across the table at her, Carlos decided there was only one thing he wanted for dessert: a taste of her lips. Yet, her viewing him as defensive didn't exactly bode well for a chance to satisfy that craving.

He remembered what she said earlier: *Carlos, I am not the enemy. We're on the same team now. Why won't you trust me?* She was so earnest reaching out to him.

Was he really going to continue to let the past rob him

of happiness? There was only one way to make sure that didn't happen.

"It's been nearly three years now," he said. "That's more than enough time for any marks to fade."

"Except for here." Bracing her elbows on the table, she reached across the small table for two and put her right hand on his heart. The gesture took him by surprise. Instinctively, he put his hand over hers.

"No, that was the first part to heal."

She didn't pull away. "I don't believe you."

He started to ask if she was calling him a liar. But after today's confession, that did seem too defensive. Maybe there was hope for him after all.

"What makes you think that?"

"You're still holding on to the past."

He drew in a deep breath and counted to ten, until he could answer without an edge to his voice.

"The only reason it came up was because you asked," he said. Her hand was warm and small in his. And he ran his thumb over her smooth skin. "And I told you."

"But you almost let it cost you an opportunity. You said yourself that you almost didn't take the job because of all that happened."

"But I took the job. And here we are."

His words seemed to catch her off guard and for a moment she wavered, uncertainty shadowing her face.

"If you hate television work so much, why *did* you take the job, Carlos?"

He shifted his grip to lace his fingers through hers.

"There are two reasons. One is simple. The other is complicated. Which one would you like to hear?"

"Both."

He nodded. *Fair enough.*

"The simple answer is, I needed the money and I'll be honest, when Chandler offered the four-episode contract—future contracts to be negotiated after he had a chance to assess the first four—" he rolled his eyes and said the words in a mocking sing-song voice "—I sort of came into this with the idea of taking the money and running after I'd fulfilled the first contract."

Lindsay's eyes flashed.

He knew it sounded crass, but it was the truth and he had to lay the truth on the table so that she could see it plain and clear. He wanted her to know he had nothing to hide.

"Really, it hasn't been so bad. Not unbearable like my first go at television. But that's beside the point."

She pulled her hand away as utter panic washed over her face. "Carlos, if you don't come back, that could mean *I'm* out of a job, too."

"The reality is Chandler holds the strings here. We could both very well be out of jobs if the show doesn't suit him. Let's cross that bridge when we come to it, okay?"

She nodded, but her eyes still held a glint of wariness. "You're right. Please continue. You were saying…"

"Yes, I was saying…do you remember that first night at dinner when I mentioned this crazy dream of mine?"

He took her hand again. This time, he stroked her palm with his thumb. The silky softness made it very hard for him to concentrate, because his mind kept drifting to how her hands would feel on his naked body—touching and caressing, possessing.…

"Prima Bella Donna was never my vision. It was Donna's. Obviously, because of the name. She never wanted children so the restaurant was her legacy. She had no desire to have kids. They would've held her back, and with the restaurant *she* was the center of attention. She rubbed elbows with celebrities like Madonna and Lenny Kravitz and was essentially the toast of South Beach. The restaurant was her baby."

Lindsay quirked a brow. "Prima Bella Donna. I get it."

He stopped stroking her palm, and he sensed her pulling back a little. "Are you sure you want to hear this?"

She waited a beat. "Yes. I need to hear this, Carlos."

There was a heartrending tenderness in her gaze. Yet, in the next moment something intense flared between them.

"At first, it was a challenge. It seemed everything I created was well received." He nodded. "For a while it was exciting to be the king of my kitchen under those circumstances. But it didn't last long. It was never enough for Donna. She had to keep pushing upward, onward. When the television opportunities came along things began to change.

"You see, I loved the part of being able to cook what I wanted to cook, and when that changed, when the media dictated my every move, I wanted to retreat into my original dream."

She leaned forward again and squeezed his hand. "What was that dream?"

He gave a nervous chuckle. He really was nervous sharing this with her. One look at the expression on her face and all discomfort evaporated.

"I always wanted to open a restaurant—nothing fancy—that offered kids who'd gotten into trouble a second chance."

Her eyes flashed with surprise. But it was good surprise. "Really?"

"Yeah." He took her hand in both of his. "My *abuela* did the best she could raising me, but like some kids with no solid male influence and too much free time out and about, I—how should I say this—had my share of run-ins with the authorities."

"So you were a bad kid, huh?"

He shrugged. "Relatively speaking. I never hurt anyone. It wasn't until I started cooking seriously that I found a true purpose. I thought about how food not only sustains, but can actually save a person's life. I'm living proof of that. I did a little research and discovered there aren't many places—and I'm talking quality places, fine dining—that offer wayward kids an opportunity to learn on the job and get their lives together.

"After the divorce, when I moved to Cedar Inlet, that's what I had in mind. To open a working restaurant that served as a training ground for troubled young adults. I want to call it Out of the Fire. It would be a teaching restaurant where the premise is you don't have to be formally trained at a hoity-toity culinary school. I'd love it if all the instructors were self-taught. The focus will be teaching these kids the basics, giving them a sense of self-worth, so that they can stand on their own two feet. But my preliminary efforts revealed two obstacles."

"What are they?"

"Zoning and, of course, money. So I put the restaurant on hold, wrote the cookbook and planned to tour until I had enough seed money to fulfill my dream. When Chandler offered me the show, the money was too good to turn down. I could accomplish in one month what it would take at least three years to rake in hawking my wares."

The waiter brought the check.

"Let me get it," Lindsay said.

He didn't even look up from the leather bill folder. "Don't be ridiculous. Besides, you picked up the last one."

Her belly did a curious spiral when she remembered what happened the last time after they'd had dinner together.

"Chandler picked up the last one," Lindsay protested, trying to keep her mind from getting carried away.

Carlos lifted his eyes and snared her gaze. "Yes, last time was business."

Oh, God. What did that mean?

She knew what it meant. People didn't hold hands across the table after a business dinner. There was absolutely nothing businesslike about this shared meal.

Unless you considered the unfinished business between them.

She'd started it earlier in the car, prodding until he opened up. Then a few minutes ago, when she'd traced the spot where his wedding ring had been; she'd known how long he'd been divorced. She'd learned about it in her initial research for *The Diva Dishes*.

She just had to make sure his head—and heart—were in the right place before…

"Come on," he said. "Let's get out of here."

He stood and helped her with her chair and coat once they got to the coat check stand.

Outside, the temperature had dropped dramatically and there were snow flurries. Lindsay shivered, and Carlos put his arm around her as they walked.

It was a fluid gesture. Natural. Not tentative or apologetic. It was as if they'd always shared this intimacy.

"So La Barbacane had a Michelin star," she said. "What did you think?"

He nodded his approval. "Delicious. Made me miss being in the kitchen, but not regret refusing the award. Cooking is my sanctuary. Having that award hanging over my head would be an albatross. It's subjective. Maybe the next year they wouldn't have understood what I was doing and they would have taken the star back. Maybe I shouldn't care."

He shook his head. "It seems pretty stupid of me, I suppose."

"No. Believe it or not, I do understand where you're coming from. Remember me telling you about my mother's recipe notebook? Baking is *my* sanctuary. When I'm stressed I bake, when I'm sad I bake. But there are no expectations. Reading my mother's writing always made me feel close to her. Even though I couldn't go to her. I mean, I never really knew her since I was so young when she died. Those recipes are a place where I can turn, without judgment. My sanctuary. I can't imagine having to strive for perfection every time I baked."

"Well, in a restaurant, the chef has an obligation to his customer. That's a given if he wants to stay in business—"

"Shh." Lindsay stopped and turned, pressing a gloved finger to Carlos's lips. "I get it. You don't have to explain."

Their faces were so close; his lips were right there. All she'd have to do is lean in a bit more… Instead, she laced her arm through his and walked on. Until Carlos stopped in front of a window with an animated display of Santa's workshop.

In the glow of the soft amber lights, she caught a glimpse of them—arm in arm, looking like a couple—in the storefront window and the sight took her breath away. Right then, she knew Chandler be dammed, they'd passed that point of question and were barreling head over heart toward the point of no return.

The only question left was, what next?

They lingered, watching the rosy-faced Santa raise and lower a "Naughty or Nice?" list as his elves busily hammered away at miniature workbenches in the background.

Carlos broke the silence. "Earlier, I mentioned there were two reasons I accepted Chandler's job offer, but I only told you one."

"What's the other reason?"

Gently, he took her by the shoulders and turned her toward him.

"The other reason was…you."

Me?

The way he gazed at her with those deep, smoldering eyes the color of dark jade turned her liquid with silken juices.

He looked at her in a way that no man had ever before. Just what did he see with that intense gaze?

When he shifted toward her and ran a finger along her jawline, suddenly it didn't matter what he saw. Because she knew he was going to kiss her. He hesitated, as if giving her a chance to pull away, but warm in his arms, the only place she wanted to be was right here.

She tilted her head and parted her lips slightly. A silent signal that she wanted him. He must have understood because he leaned in and kissed her, moving slowly at first, only brushing her lips with the most delicate of glances. He was a gentleman, no wandering hands. He simply rested one on her shoulder and the other on her arm, as if he waited for her to kiss him back.

Her heartbeat pounded in her rib cage, until slowly, almost cautiously, she leaned into the kiss. Her breath quickened as she surrendered to shivers of heat and need.

When she sucked at his bottom lip, it was as if she'd turned the burners on a gas range on high. Heat and need exploded and his body responded.

But as much as he burned to pull her against him, to explore her body with his hands until she turned to dough in his hands, as much as he wanted to sweep her up in his arms and into one of the Carcassonne hotels and take off her clothes and run his tongue over every inch of her supple body, he resisted. He stood there, steeling himself as he let her set the pace.

He didn't want either of them walking away with regrets this time.

When she nipped at his bottom lip, this time he angled his head to the side and parted his lips for her. As she slipped her tongue into his mouth, his body got hotter, harder, his need more intense. It was all he could do to keep his hands off her, to not take her by the hand and lead her into one of the alleyways and back her against the wall of one of these ancient buildings and make love to her then and there. Need consumed him, threatened to overwhelm him, but they were finally meeting on solid ground, mutual ground, and he was determined not to mess things up this time.

But when she deepened the kiss and sighed, it took every bit of self-control he had not to crush her to him. Instead he held his ground, kissing her back slowly, gently without unleashing the all-consuming passion that fired through his blood. And he waited for her to be the one to pull back first. When she did, gasping for breath, he steadied himself by cupping her face in his hands, touching her to make sure this kiss in this storybook city was real and not a dream.

It was real all right. The excruciating pleasure-pain of his rock-hard erection was proof of exactly how real.

As they made their way to the car, arm in arm, he felt scorching hot despite the cold. He tightened his grip on Lindsay, pulling her snug against his side, needing to feel her body against his. In time, the need to bury himself inside her would ease to a bearable level. His arousal would ease to a dull, aching throb until, in good time, they'd finish what they'd started.

And that *finish* would be the start of something brand-new.

When they reached the car, he bent down and kissed her again. The parking lot was dark and he was warm, and for a moment Lindsay got lost in the feel of his lips moving over hers.

Only for a moment. Because if it would've been more than a moment, she might have gotten completely lost and never found her way back.

"Carlos," she breathed, pulling away slightly from the kiss. "There are so many reasons why this is a bad idea."

He leaned in and found her lips again. "Bad idea…?" he said around the kiss.

"Mmm-hmm… We have to work together."

He ran his tongue over her lower lip.

"Work? Right now?"

She bit down lightly on his lower lip.

"No, silly, not right now. But tomorrow, and, I hope, many days after that."

She heard herself saying the words, but she couldn't find the strength to pull out of his arms. To focus directly on the conversation. Even though she knew she should.

"You know, talking is highly overrated. We do enough of that on camera. Right now it's just you and me and all this chemistry Chandler keeps talking about."

"Exactly. I don't want to mess this up...." Her voice shook.

He dropped his hands to her hips, and pulled her in close. Trailing his lips down her jawline to a place behind her ear, he kissed her in a way that made her lose her train of thought.

"I think we're far from messing this up. We're *so* good at this. I don't think we could mess up if we tried." He whispered this into her ear before sucking on her lobe, sending shivers of pleasure throughout her body.

"No, Carlos, really. It's happened to me before."

He flinched a little.

But there, she'd done it. He raised his head and squinted down at her.

"What's happened to you before?" He loosened his hold on her.

For a moment, she warred with herself. Why had she brought this up? No, she knew that answer. Knew she had to do it. This job was her chance to get on with her life. To make something of herself. To be the person her father always hoped she'd be. With all this at stake, why was she falling right back into the old trap again?

"Getting involved with a coworker and it turning out badly." The words made her cringe.

Especially when his body tightened and a strange,

confused half smile quirked up his lips. "Coworker? Is that that what we are, coworkers?"

His hands fell to his side.

Of course this wasn't going to be easy. Dredging up the past never was. But he'd had the guts to lay his past wide-open, she needed to do the same.

"Well, technically, yes. Because we do work together. The future of the show relies on us...and if we... And it doesn't work out...Chandler will—"

"I don't give a damn what Chandler thinks. When we're off the clock, what we do with our time is nobody's business but our own. That's the problem I had from the beginning."

"But you don't understand, I can't make that mistake again."

"I am not *that* mistake, Lindsay."

"You don't know what happened."

"No, I don't. There's no way I will unless you tell me."

She sighed. "Let's get in the car."

And then she began. "When I was just out of college, I landed a reporting job at WKMO, a TV station in Charleston. I met and fell in love with a man who was one of their star reporters. He was vying for an anchor position. We eventually got engaged, but Derrick wanted to keep the engagement quiet. He seemed to think that he'd be more 'attractive' and promotable if he was unencumbered. In this business, family is seen as a liability—they want young, attractive free agents who are willing to move at the drop of a hat—or so he said. And yes, that was the air around the station. Movers and shakers who were all in a friendly competition to be the next one to climb up to the next rung. If a nose job made you more attractive, you had your nose done. If hiding your engagement made you more salable, you had a secret engagement. Boy, was I stupid…." She shook her head, embarrassed by how gullible she must seem.

"But of course, people knew Derrick and I were seeing each other. There was no law prohibiting interoffice romance. In fact, the pairings often shifted depending on who was coming and going. So since we weren't very private about our romantic relationship, my boss decided I must have been a player and decided to test me to see how badly I wanted to move up. I was young and stupid and thought I was in love. So basically, I told him to keep his hands off me and when it was clear he wouldn't take me seriously, I lodged a sexual harassment complaint against him.

"Long story short, because I was 'sleeping with' Derrick, as he put it, he made me out to be the station tramp. He even got others to lie and say I'd slept with them, which was totally false. Lies. I was in love. I was going to get married….

"But when it came down to it, Derrick distanced himself. You see it was the promotion or me. And suddenly I was a pariah. He broke the engagement, and then—surprise, surprise—my contract wasn't renewed the following year.

"Lies cost me my job and my fiancé. Go ahead and say it. I'm sure you're wondering how I could've been so blind. So stupid not to have seen it coming. How do you find yourself engaged to a man who, in the end, you didn't even know? Believe me, I've asked myself that same question every single day over the past seven years. How could I have been so blind? It's caused me to question my judgment and every single man I meet."

Carlos held up both hands. "I am the last person who would ever judge you. Yeah, me, the jester of Prima Bella Donna's court."

They were quiet for a moment. The stillness was vibrant with confession.

"But think about it," he finally said. "Aren't you glad you didn't marry him? I know you went through hell, but it sounds like the situation may have saved you from a bad marriage."

She frowned, not quite on the same page as Carlos. "Yeah, but it was a pretty high price to pay. Don't you think?"

"And a bad marriage is no picnic, either. Take it from someone who knows. And just so you're clear with it, I think it's abominable that he threw you over like that. What kind of a man won't stand up for his fiancée? I'm not Derrick."

No, he wasn't. He couldn't be further apart from Derrick. She'd known him such a short period of time and already she felt as if she knew more about Carlos than she'd known about a man to whom she was ready to pledge the rest of her life.

Bad judgment.

"There does come a time when you have to stop blaming yourself," he said. "I've been through it. So I know."

He started the car and turned on the radio. On the long drive back to Toulouse, neither of them said much. Instead, they listened to the plaintive French tunes that emanated from the speakers. She didn't understand most of what they sang, but the songs filled the silence and gave her time to think.

Now that everything was out on the table, the similarity of their situations was a little eerie. Both of them had been burned by people they'd loved and trusted. Both had lived through the decimation of their careers and were just starting to come out on the other side. Now here they were, two broken, battered souls, trying to make their way the best they knew how.

Brutal honesty was one way to kill a budding romance. But at least she'd saved her job this time.

Regret—for having said too much, for having chased him off—sat like a rock in the pit of her stomach. She felt a little shaky as she tried to convince herself that having shared so much with him was for the best. It was sort of like she'd run an emotional marathon. She hurt now, but in the days to come she'd feel stronger and better for having done it.

Only right now the voice inside her screamed, *What the hell were you thinking?*

They pulled into the Leblanc Inn parking lot about an hour later.

"Here we are." He killed the engine and turned to her. "It's been…quite a day."

She nodded, completely drained of words.

"You know," he said, "they only win if we let them."

So easy to say. So much harder to do.

"After tomorrow's shoot, we're off until after the new year. Why don't we prove to ourselves how far we've come? Lindsay, come to Paris with me. Let's spend the holidays together."

Her first instinct was to leave. Fast. But it was too late. She'd already let him in.

Chapter Thirteen

Paris for the holidays. How could she resist?

Her first reaction had been to say no.

But along with the romantic notion came a whole host of questions. It sounded too ridiculous to ask what his intentions were—the guy had nearly kissed her pants off in public. She'd managed to exercise good judgment and get to her room—alone—that night, but if she spent ten days alone with him in Paris, she wasn't sure she'd be so strong. She wasn't sure she wanted to because all logic had been completely undone by the memory of Carlos's kiss and the pull of a feeling that simply wouldn't go away—no matter how she tried to distance herself from him.

A feeling that she was quite possibly falling in love with him. That she'd already fallen.

The realization hit her hard. She didn't know when

it had manifested—during the kiss or the first moment their eyes met at the wedding.

It simply was. As if it had been rooted inside her always, lying dormant until now.

It was a timeless feeling, as primal and organic as the earth and the oceans and the sky.

This was different than anything she'd experienced before and she had no idea what she was going to do about it. Except that the best place to try and find out was in Paris.

The left-bank apartment belonged to Carlos's friend, Paul, whose job had taken him to Istanbul for three months. When Carlos called to tell him he'd be in Paris for the holidays, Paul had insisted he stay there.

"I'll leave word with the concierge," Paul had said. "He'll have a key for you."

Situated on a charming cobblestone street in Paris's Latin Quarter, it was a welcome change from the hotels Carlos had been living in since Max had arranged the book tour.

As Carlos took their bags out of the tiny, mirrored lift, which was barely large enough for the two of them and their luggage, he caught a glimpse of Lindsay's reflection. Her long, blond hair hung in loose curls around her shoulders. It looked like spun gold contrasted with her black knit beret and wool coat. Her cheeks were blushed pink from the cold night and her brown eyes looked dark and seductive in the half-light of the elevator.

Her beauty astounded him, or maybe it was the fact that they were here together in Paris.

Her gaze snared his in the mirror. "Is this our stop?"

"It is." He cleared his throat, inexplicably nervous. *Did someone just turn up the heat?*

They found unit 294. He unlocked the door, then held it open for her to enter first. As she moved past him, he breathed in her scent, an action that had become almost reflexive when she was near—breathing her in, wanting to experience as much of her as possible. One hand on the doorknob, he shoved the other in his coat pocket to keep himself from reaching out and pulling her into his arms.

With its tall, beamed ceilings and rough-hewn plank floors, the apartment was gorgeous. A door at the end of a small hallway opened into a bathroom. The other two doors were bedrooms.

Two bedrooms.

Carlos simply set both bags in the hallway.

"Look at this," Lindsay called from the living room.

She was standing at one of the large windows looking out. "You can see the Seine from here. Let's go take a walk."

It was just a short walk, less than five minutes, from the apartment to the river. They both remained silent, listening to the cars whir past and the sounds of Paris after dark.

The cold night air was invigorating. The City of Love was all around her and Carlos was next to her, reaching for her hand.

Why she was so anxious? It was too late to change her mind, she thought as he laced his fingers through hers. Well, it was never too late to decide *not* to sleep with a man. It was every woman's prerogative to say no right up to the last second.

The problem wasn't that she didn't want him. In fact, it was her feelings that made this situation so impossible. She also wanted her job. She needed her job. She was just getting her life on the right track and then she had to go and fall in love.

He led her down the steps of the quay, and there they were—standing along the Seine River. Water lapped against the embankment and lights danced across the rippled surface like a moody Impressionist painting come to life before her very eyes.

What if things didn't work out? What if he changed his mind about how he felt about her? They'd still have to work together. Memories of Derrick flashed through her mind.

She'd thought she'd had it all then, too. The perfect job, the perfect man…then one day she woke up and it was all gone.

It had changed the direction of her life. Yet she'd let herself get swept away again. This wasn't a vacation romance.

"Are you okay?" Carlos dropped her hand and slid his arm around her, pulling her in close. "Is it too cold for you?"

She shivered a little, but shook her head.

The power of suggestion.

"*Nah,* just tired, I think."

There was nothing like an open-air Parisian market. The array of fresh baked bread, vegetables, meats, cheeses and wine was a chef's dream. Succulent white asparagus. Ripe blueberries, strawberries, blackberries and raspberries. Artichokes so fat and healthy Carlos could almost taste them…mmm…served with lemon-garlic aioli.

It was more than a dream.

It was nirvana.

He'd gotten the fixings for coq au vin. With mashed garlic-leek potatoes and green beans, it was the ultimate comfort food.

Just what Lindsay needed.

Earlier, she'd baked her mom's Ultimate Cookies for dessert.

They were the most incredible and delicious of any sweet he'd ever tasted. When he first bit into the chewy goodness, he had visions of living happily with just Lindsay, a bed and an endless supply of her Ultimate Cookies.

They were an absolute aphrodisiac.

But then again, it was the first time they'd cooked together. There was something sexy about the process of working side-by-side in the kitchen. He wished they could simply ditch the rest of the show and live in this private culinary bubble from now on.

But...he would honor his commitment.

The press might say a lot of bad things about him, but one thing he prided himself in was upholding his commitments.

He uncorked a bottle of Volnay and poured two glasses, one of which he handed to Lindsay. After they clinked goblets, he lifted his and savored its bouquet of red berries and violet. It would be delicious with the chicken. It was great to be in the kitchen again. He missed moments like this, shopping for and cooking a good meal; pairing just the right wine to go with the dish. To him these were life's simplest pleasures.

Lindsay sat at the bar that divided the kitchen and living room. "I've always wondered how to make coq au vin."

Carlos furrowed his brow. "Oh, it's terribly difficult."

"Really?"

He pulled several sprigs of the fresh thyme he'd purchased, then held them under cool running water.

"No, actually it's quite simple. The secret to a good coq au vin is to use good wine and let it take its time cooking so that all the ingredients have a chance to meld."

He put butter in a sauté pan and turned on the stove's burner. The flame ignited with a *poof,* and immediately the butter began to sizzle and slide around the pan.

"Let me teach you how," he said. "That way you'll have a wonderful dinner to add to your repertoire."

"I guess a repertoire has to start with a first recipe."

He did a double take. "What? You don't cook for yourself?"

She shook her head. "I bake. I didn't make any claims about cooking."

"How do you subsist?"

She shrugged. "I manage, I guess."

"Come in here," he said. "I want to teach you how to make this."

"How can I resist a private lesson?" She slid off the stool and appeared in the kitchen. The overhead light brought out the gold in her hair. Yet her porcelain skin seemed to glow from within. She stood so close to him, if his hands hadn't been full of pearl onions, he would've reached out and taken her into his arms. He did the second best thing; he listed to the right until their shoulders touched.

"First, we're going to blanch the onions in boiling water," he said. "That'll help the skin to slide right off."

She reached out and took one of the small bulbs from his hand, and her pinkie trailed along his palm. She looked up snared his gaze.

"Onions, huh? I don't want to cry again."

He set down the onions and took her face in his hands.

"I promise you, I won't make you cry, Lindsay. I am not Derrick."

They stared at each other as the truth of the moment closed in around them. They'd set aside the posturing and their guards had fallen, letting in an intimacy that was so deep, so intense, it stung.

They'd shared their most personal secrets. They knew the worst and the best of each other. Even though it scared him to think of caring for someone that much, he'd already passed the point of no return. There was no denying the truth. He'd fallen for her…hard.

The only question was, where did they go from here?

She must have read the question on his face, because she answered it by turning off the stove burners, then leaning in and kissing him. He responded by pulling her in closer and wrapping his arms around her as if he'd never let her go.

Every inch of her body was pressed against his. He lost himself in the heated tenderness of their embrace.

He knew instinctively that she'd be a decisive lover. The way her hands explored his body—his shoulders, his back, his waist. Her touch excited him and promised that she'd claim him with a need that just might leave him even more defenseless than he was now. If that was possible.

In response, he wanted to show her how much he ached for her, how he'd longed for this moment since the night he'd first laid eyes on her. Rather than using words, he conveyed his feelings as his lips claimed hers in a kiss meant to sear her soul.

Desire grew as he held her and tasted her. In response his own body swelled and hardened. He loved the feel of her curves, supple to his touch. When he dropped his hands to her hips and pulled her closer, she arched against him, fueling the hardness of his desire.

"I want you," she murmured breathlessly.

He raised his hands to her breasts, cupping them, memorizing her curves before teasing her hard nipples. She gasped. Her head dropped back and she seemed to lose herself in his touch.

Then it was his turn. She slid her hand down the front of his jeans and claimed his erection. Over and over she teased him, rubbing and stroking his desire through the layers of his jeans and briefs. The sensation was almost too much to bear. So he backed away a little, leaning in to kiss the side of her neck, playfully biting down on her earlobe.

In anticipation of their lovemaking, a shudder racked his whole body. Suddenly he needed her naked so that he could bury himself inside of her.

She must have wanted the same thing, because in one swift move, she began to unbuckle the button on his jeans, slid down the zipper and pushed his briefs to the floor. He stepped out of both, and shrugged off his shirt, unashamed of his nakedness.

Wanting to permanently imprint her on his senses, he deliberately slowed down and undid each button on her shirt. Pushing it away, he unhooked the front clasp on her bra. As he freed her breasts, he lowered his head and, in turn, took each one into his mouth, suckling them until she cried out in pleasure. Then, when he was sure she was ready, he tugged down her trousers and panties.

As they stood together naked, despite the need

driving him to the edge of madness, again, he purposely slowed down, taking a moment to commit to memory the way her beautiful body looked.

And then they were reaching for each other and touching everywhere, a tangle of arms and legs.

"Let's go into the bedroom," she murmured.

He kissed her deeply as he backed her down the hall—tongues thrusting, hands exploring, teeth nipping. A sensual *pas de deux* that led them to a bedroom. He wasn't really cognizant of which one, but was only aware of laying her down on the bed.

"Now," she said. And he buried himself inside her.

Their vacation in Paris was what Lindsay liked to call a *snow globe moment*: a picture-perfect vignette suspended in time.

Oh, how she wished she really could stop time so that she and Carlos could live inside that bubble forever. It was the most romantic ten days of her life, and their time together went by as quickly as the snow settled in a shaken snow globe.

They spent a romantic Christmas together cooking a traditional stuffed goose. They'd even purchased a small tree at the open-air market on the rue Cler, which they decorated and lit on Christmas Eve before they'd eaten and exchanged gifts.

Carlos surprised her with a hand-tooled leather journal. "Your mother's book has meant so much to you. Now, it's time you started your own."

The gesture brought tears to her eyes. For a moment, she thought she'd come undone. Never had such a simple gift held such meaning and possibility. It made the vintage brass bowl she'd found for him at one of the open-air markets seem insignificant in comparison. But he made it seem as if the gift was perfect.

They rang in the new year drinking champagne and making love until dawn. Lindsay would've been perfectly happy to stay naked in his arms for the rest of the year. Alas, soon enough reality came calling, shattering their snow globe existence and forcing them back into the real world: they had to go back to work.

Except for Max, none of the cast and crew knew that Lindsay and Carlos had spent the holidays together. They'd decided it would probably be best if they kept their relationship a secret.

At least until after they negotiated the new contract with Chandler.

That seemed like the smart thing to do. Especially when, on the first day back, Chandler called a breakfast meeting with the two of them in his hotel suite.

He'd ordered in a variety of pastries and fruit, coffee and tea. They expected the reason for the meeting was to talk about their contracts since the Paris shoot was the fourth and final shoot on the current contract.

As they settled in with their plates, he asked, "Did you have a nice Christmas?"

"Yes." Lindsay sipped her coffee. Her mind raced to come up with a plausible explanation as to how she'd spent the holidays, if he asked. A natural overview, without giving away too much—and without lying to Chandler.

"How about you, Carlos?"

Carlos bit into his pastry. He nodded furiously, pointing to his mouth, playing the old can't-talk-with-food-in-my-mouth card.

Chandler looked back and forth between them. "Well, it looks to me like you had quite a romantic time."

He took a folder off the end table next to his chair and began to flip through a stack of eight-by-ten photographs.

"I see you made it to the Eiffel Tower."

What? Lindsay sat frozen, afraid to even glance at Carlos.

"And the Louvre." He held up another of them embracing on the rue du Rivoli, the street that ran along the north wing of the museum. "Did you happen to make it to the Musée Marmottan? It always seems to live in the shadow of the larger, better-known Parisian museums. But your walk along the Seine looked particularly romantic."

Lindsay's chest tightened as he held up photo after photo chronicling their holiday.

"In the future, you might want to be more aware of who's following you. Now that you're on television, there are always cameras about. Paparazzi looking to make a buck."

But the show hadn't even aired yet.

"What we do on our own time is our business." Carlos spat the words.

"Your business and anyone who cares to look at CelebrityLoveFest.com. That's where these came from."

Chandler tossed the photos onto the coffee table and they scattered in different directions.

She and Carlos each grabbed a photo off the table. The caption on the one Lindsay held said, *Former Food TV bad boy Carlos Montigo has signed on with a new network to host a brand-new show called* The Diva Drives. *He and his Diva cohost, Lindsay Bingham, were spotted together heating up Paris. Maybe Montigo is no longer yesterday's leftovers.*

Lindsay's blood pounded and her face grew hot with humiliation. Especially when Carlos flung the photo he'd been looking at back onto the table.

"You can't dictate what we do when we're not filming, Chandler." There was an edge to Carlos's voice. Lindsay slanted a glance at him. His expression matched his tone.

Chandler's face darkened. "The only reason I'm not arguing that point is because this isn't bad publicity for the show."

He and Carlos stared at each other. Two alpha males in a standoff.

"Everybody loves a love affair. So, as long as this generates good publicity for the show, I have no problem with it. But the minute it starts interfering it'll be a different story."

Carlos stiffened.

"Nowhere in the contract does it mention anything about you dictating our personal lives."

Chandler folded his hands in his lap. "That's covered by the morals clause. Believe me, Mr. Montigo, when it comes to business, I leave nothing to chance."

Chapter Fourteen

There were few things that Carlos hated more than feeling owned. In fact, right about now, he couldn't think of a single thing that irked him more.

Except, perhaps, Chandler using Carlos's and Lindsay's relationship to further his business interests. Sure, common sense dictated that in this case Chandler's business interests benefited Carlos. They were banking on the show getting off on the right foot so that Chandler would extend the contract.

However, even that was up in the air for the time being. Chandler said the fate of the full season was still in limbo because he was still negotiating with sponsors. Something about it sounded like a flimsy excuse. They were in their last week of the pilot, and surely Chandler would've known by now if he was going to continue with the show.

Max had ensured him there was no need to worry. He'd make sure these *negotiations* didn't drag on too long. Right now, Carlos didn't know if he wanted to sign his life away for a full season. The money from the pilot was enough seed money to go back to Cedar Inlet and open his restaurant. After this week's shoot, he would've fulfilled his contractual obligation to Chandler. Then he'd be free to tell him what he could do with his morals clause. The only thing stopping him was Lindsay.

Carlos's walking away would affect her, too. He didn't know what he was going to do about the situation. But Chandler hadn't yet put the new contracts on the table, so there was no sense in worrying about it until he had to commit to signing his life away.

In the meantime, it was more important to him to prove to Lindsay that despite how much he hated the prying media and Chandler's assertions of ownership, the bad situation had not changed his feelings for her one bit.

That's why he'd worked with Paula to arrange an on-camera surprise for Lindsay on their third day of shooting.

"Here, put this on." The cameras were rolling as Carlos and Lindsay sat in Bella. He handed her a red silk scarf.

She laughed. "What is this, a scarf-tying test? Just because we're in Paris does not automatically mean I've become scarf-savvy. Even if this is an Hermès scarf. *Ooh,* this is nice—"

"It's a nice blindfold." He took the silk fabric from her hands. "I want you to put it on because I have a surprise for you."

Thoughts of the things they could do with a silk scarf and a four-poster bed flashed through his head and blood rushed south and pooled in his groin.

He shifted. It wasn't the time for that. Reaching over, he gently tied the scarf over her eyes.

"Carlos, are you sure this is absolutely necessary?"

"Absolutely." He gave the camera his most devastating grin before he steered Bella out of the parking space.

"Where are you taking me?"

"If I told you, it wouldn't be a surprise, would it?"

She looked sexy with the silk tied over her eyes, the wind tousling the ends of her blond hair about her shoulders.

He only had a short distance to drive and a few minutes later Carlos stopped in front of a small bakery.

"Stay right here," he said. "I'll be around to help you out of the car. And don't peek."

A small crowd gathered outside as the cameras filmed Carlos helping Lindsay from the car and into the bakery.

"Okay," he said. "You can remove the blindfold."

Even with her eyes covered, the first thing that hit Lindsay once she stepped inside out of the cold was a luscious mélange of sweet aromas—fresh-baked bread, almond paste, chocolate and strong-brewed coffee.

Her mouth watered. *Mmm...* Her favorite smells. Maybe this segment was a pastry tasting…or a spot on the best boulangeries in Paris? But why the blindfold? Well, whatever it was, if it involved French pastry she wanted in.

She pulled the scarf from her eyes and blinked as she looked around a stunning Art Deco-style pâtisserie, complete with starburst light fixtures, 1930s-era mirrors, marble counter tops and a curved brass and glass display case.

It was gorgeous. If she ever opened a place of her own this is what it would look like.

The cameras were rolling as Carlos and a rotund man in a crisp white apron stood next to her, smiling as if they knew the punch line to a joke Lindsay wasn't yet aware of. Though she had a feeling they'd enlighten her soon enough.

"It's a tightly kept secret that one of Lindsay's passions is baking," Carlos winked at the camera. "But I happen to believe she makes the best cookies *anyone* has ever tasted. Today we wanted to put that to the test and surprise her by introducing her to the man who was voted Paris's best pastry chef, Rene Delanoë."

Lindsay stood blank, amazed and not quite sure how she felt about her secret love of baking being revealed to the world. It had always been private, something she turned to when she was sad or lonely or otherwise needed cheering up. Something that connected her to her mother.

But, wow. Rene Delanoë. She'd heard of him and his world-famous Pâtisserie Delanoë.

Had Carlos arranged this for her?

Sure, it was for the show. What was a trip to Paris without a sweet treat? But he could've just set it up in the same way they set up all the segments.

He'd obviously gone to a lot of trouble to make this a surprise. And that warmed her from the inside out.

"A *pâtisserie* is a French bakery that specializes in pastries and sweets," Carlos said. "In France, it is an official title that only bakeries employing a *maître pâtissier*—or master pastry chef—may use. The Pâtisserie Delanoë is actually both a *pâtisserie* and a *boulangerie*, right?"

It was awkward standing there mute. Even though she hadn't had the benefit of preparing for the segment, Lindsay decided it was better to jump in than say nothing. "What's the difference between the two, chef?"

"A *boulangerie* specializes in bread," said Delanoë in heavily accented English. "A *pâtisserie* is about the sweets."

"While we're here, Chef Delanoë is going to show us how he makes his world-famous madeleines," said Carlos. "We'll try to wrangle the secret recipe out of him. And speaking of secret recipes, I'm going to see if I can't convince Lindsay to treat us all to the incomparable treat of her Ultimate Cookies. What do you say, Linds?"

She knew the recipe by heart. But she'd never really put it to the test.

"Hmm..." she stalled. "Well, this is quite a surprise. Why do I get the feeling if I say anything other than yes that you'll tie me to a chair with that scarf until I agree?"

The thought sent butterflies swooping in her stomach, but that was nothing compared to the way her body reacted when he quirked his brow and flashed that devastating smile of his.

"Now there's an idea. But before we get too distracted, Rene is going to give us a tour of the pastry case over here."

Lindsay trailed behind Carlos, following the siren song of his broad shoulders over to the glass case.

"Who needs any other enticement?" she said wistfully.

Reluctantly, she tore her gaze away and focused on the artful array of sweet decadence in front of her: tarts in nearly any flavor one could name—even chestnut; rustic, free-form fruit tarts that begged to be tasted; cakes of all shapes and sizes that looked more like works of art than sugary confections: Napoleon, chocolate *rhum* and something called a Hippodrome, which was decorated with meringue, almonds and apricot glaze. *Ooh*...then there were the chocolate éclairs, the Choux Chantilly and Praline Riviera....

"Could I have one of each, please?"

"But of course." With a wave of his hand, Delanoë's assistant began assembling a sampler platter, as the chef moved on to introduce a range of specialty breads: baguettes, boules, ficelles and fougasse, which Delanoë explained was a ladder-shaped loaf doused with olive oil and baked with fillings that changed daily—black olives one day, chèvre and tomatoes the next. Then there were the croissants, decadently plump, with a golden exterior that looked as if it would flake at the slightest touch.

"And over here we have the ever popular *pain au chocolat,*" said Delanoë. "It is sort of, how you say, a bridge between the bread and the sweets. We use the best possible chocolate. Good quality is a must. We will not settle for less.

"You see, not all *chocolat* is created equal. True, it is all made from cacao beans, which are from the Theobroma tree. Did you know that *Theobroma* translates to 'Food of the Gods'? That's probably because of its great aphrodisiac qualities." He wiggled his bushy gray brows at Lindsay.

Paula called, "Cut. That's a perfect note to end on. Because we'd planned on giving some details on where chocolate comes from. We were going to do this in a chocolate shop, but it looks like the shooting schedule will be a little tight. I think we'll cut that and expand on the patisserie. Lindsay, you'll do a voice-over, which we'll dub as we transition from the front of the house into the kitchen. Why don't you do a quick read-through of what's on the cue cards?"

"Sure."

Paula held up the cards and Lindsay recited:

"The type and blend of cacao beans and where they are grown all contribute to the final quality and taste of the chocolate. Other factors are how the beans are grown and ultimately roasted, and how they're processed.

"Here's a bit of trivia for you. Did you know there are three types of cacao beans? The forastero, criollo and trinitario.

"The most important point to consider when choosing the chocolate with which you will bake is whether you like the taste of the chocolate when you eat it in its unmelted form. Come on, let's go into the kitchen and see what the chef has cooking."

Despite the freezing temperatures and one rainy day, the Paris shoot went by nearly seamlessly.

Lindsay prepared her mother's cookie recipe for Chef Delanoë, and he proclaimed it "magnifique," with a quiet reverence that spoke volumes. He even asked her to share her recipe. She wouldn't, because it was an old family recipe. Even so, he said she had a job working with him at Pâtisserie Delanoë if she ever wanted a career change.

"That's very nice of you," she said.

"No, no, no," he said. "Make no mistake. I am never simply *nice.* Not when it comes to business. When I say you have talent, I mean it. You seem to have a knack for taking ordinary ingredients that when mixed together are," he scrunched up his face and waved his hand in a circular motion, "they are usually fine, but your seem to possess a special sensibility that allows you to make magic."

He was right about that, Carlos thought. Lindsay Bingham's touch was magic. In more ways than one.

"Maybe it's my mother baking through me?" She'd laughed it off. "Nah, baking is something I enjoy. I've been experimenting with it for so long, it's second nature."

"Well, you have a standing job offer at my patisserie."

At that moment, the irony of Delanoë's offer escaped them. It would be three days later, on their last day of shooting, when Max dropped the bomb.

They were taping the final segment for the last *Diva* episode—a nighttime picnic on the Champ de Mars, the lawn that stretches between the Eiffel Tower and École Militaire—in the freezing cold, but since the spot had to be timeless, they had to pretend like the weather was bearable.

The Eiffel Tower light show was in full flash in the background, Lindsay and Carlos were enjoying a baguette, cheese and some wine on a blue-and-white checked picnic blanket.

"The perfect ending to a perfect visit to Paris," Lindsay said as they clinked glasses. "See you next time on *The Diva Drives.*"

"Cut!" said Chandler. "We got it. Good show. That's a wrap, everyone! I'll see everyone at Jules Verne, the restaurant on the second level of the Eiffel Tower at ten."

The sixteen-member crew murmured good words and milled about, gathering up cords and equipment.

"I'm going to go back to the hotel and freshen up before the party," said Lindsay. "I'll meet you there."

"I'll ride back with you," Carlos said.

As he started to walk with her to the car, Chandler put a hand on Carlos's shoulder. "Actually, I was hoping you had a minute. I need to talk to you about something."

When Max walked up, Carlos figured it must have something to do with the new contract.

"Sure," he said to Chandler. "Lindsay, I'll walk you to the car."

"You don't have to do that. In fact, I think Paula's going that way. I'll walk with her. See you later."

Carlos squeezed her hand and watched her walk away before turning back to Chandler and Max.

"So, what's up?"

Max and Chandler exchanged a look that didn't bode well.

"What?" Carlos insisted.

"I hate to put a damper on things." Max raked a hand through his hair, a familiar nervous tic. "But I got a call from a writer for a small tabloid out of Barcelona. It seems they're working on a story."

Every muscle in Carlos's body tensed. Judging by the look on Max's face, it wasn't positive.

"Good press?" he said sarcastically.

Max scowled. "That depends on your definition of *good.* Some diehards believe *any* press is good press."

Carlos uttered an oath.

Max held up a hand. "Now wait, before you jump to conclusions, let's put it in perspective."

"Put *what* into perspective?" Carlos glanced at Chandler, who was standing there so silently it was creeping him out. Carlos fisted his hands. "What kind of muck are the scumbags raking now?"

"It's just an insignificant tabloid," Max continued as if he hadn't heard him. "A minor player in Spanish gossip."

Carlos leveled him with a glare. "Quit beating around the damn bush and tell me."

Max sucked in a breath and blew it out noisily. "They've been doing some digging into your past. They're making an issue out of an old arrest record."

For a moment, Carlos didn't know whether to laugh or put his fist through a wall. Thank God there wasn't a wall nearby. He settled for gritting his teeth and closing his eyes against the white-hot anger surging through his veins.

"You've got to be *kidding me,*" he hissed. "I was fourteen years old when it happened."

"What did you…*do* to warrant assault charges?" Chandler looked like he was sucking on a lemon. Of course. He was worried he'd made a mistake and hired a felon. Surely guys like Chandler did background checks before they invested in an employee. Then again, this probably wouldn't have come up in a background check since Carlos was so young when it happened…and the charges were bogus.

"I was caught driving a delivery truck without a license. I lived in a small village and the cop who caught me had an ax to grind with my mother." He shrugged. "When she was alive, she seemed to have that affect on men, but that's another story."

He hadn't counted on the rush of emotion that accompanied this unexpected trip down memory lane. He cleared his throat, hoping to clear the knot that had lodged there. Poker faced, Chandler stared at him, while Max shifted uncomfortably.

"I'll level with you, man. The scumbag is asking questions about your mother's drinking and your childhood. Look, we don't have to get into this here." Max gestured to the people—some crew, some tourists—milling about. "This is a delicate subject. Why don't we go back to the hotel where we can discuss this privately?"

Carlos shook his head. "There's not that much left to say. We might as well finish it here."

"Well, if you'd rather go somewhere else—" Chandler said, glancing around.

"No, I said this was fine. It'll be out soon enough. The long and short of it is, when the cop saw it was me, he tried to rough me up a bit and suddenly the driving-without-a-license charge morphed into assault and resisting arrest charges. It was all bogus. Everything was eventually dropped, but somehow money-hungry reporters can always dig up those sensational headlines, can't they."

Max looked away and cleared his throat.

"He's suggesting that maybe your rough past is a contributing factor to why you lied about your culinary background. Basically, the gist of the article seems to be that's what is at the root of your psyche."

White-hot anger simmered in his gut. He was a pressure cooker ready to blow. "So now they're trying to expose my psyche? Saying I covered up my past to avoid exposing the fact that I was raised by an abusive drunk of a mother?"

As if putting his private life on trial in the tabloids wasn't entertainment enough, now they wanted his soul. Again. Leaving him obliged to defend himself.

He watched all the people walking by, going about their happy, anonymous lives because no one gave a damn what they did when they were fourteen or thirty-four; whether they punched a crooked cop who said foul things about their mother or refused a restaurant rating.

He envied them and their anonymity. He wouldn't wish life in the public eye on his worst enemy.

"Well, I'm sure Max can handle the reporter," Chandler was saying, but Carlos could barely hear him over the blood rushing in his ears.

"Listen, I have to go."

"Are you okay?" Max asked.

"We'll see you later at the party?" Chandler said.

Carlos just turned and walked away.

When Max relayed the situation with the tabloid, Lindsay's first thought was that Carlos simply needed a some time alone to process everything, but when the dinner plates were cleared and there was still no sign of him, she started to worry. As the restaurant staff served dessert, she excused herself to go call him. She ran into him in the lobby.

"Carlos, are you okay? You missed dinner."

He looked dark and drawn. There was a long pause before he said, "Yeah, I'm not in a very festive mood tonight. I probably shouldn't have come. I'm sure Max told you what's going on?"

She nodded and touched his arm. "I'm sorry."

He stiffened and pulled back. It was an almost imperceptible flinch, but it happened, and his withdrawal stung.

"Yeah, well, I guess that's how it goes in this business," he said.

"Do you want to talk about it?" She shifted her weight from one foot to another. She'd worn the Jimmy Choo heels for the last day of the shoot, and after a sixteen-hour day her feet hated her for it, but that was nothing compared to the way her heart ached seeing him like this.

He crossed his arms and his face shuttered. "Not really."

"Come on, let's go for a walk anyway." Despite her aching feet, the best thing they could do was go somewhere so they could be alone and they could talk this out.

He hesitated, drawing in a deep breath as if preparing to protest.

"The mood you're in, do you really want to go in there?" she asked.

He smiled, but there was no humor in his eyes.

"Let me get my coat," she said, "and then let's get out of here."

When she returned, he was standing at the bank of elevators. He'd already pushed the call button.

It was just the two of them alone in the elevator. The silence was deafening. She'd never seen Carlos like this—not even earlier in the week when Chandler told them about the photographs. She'd caught glimpses of his stoic media animosity when she'd asked questions during their initial interview and when he finally opened up about the past, but it paled in comparison to this silent simmering anger.

Common sense told her his mood wasn't directed at her, but it was hard not to take it a little personally. Even so…maybe if she could just get him talking about it—

"We haven't even talked about what happens next?" His question surprised her.

Next? As in them? Together?

Or as in them as coworkers?

"I don't know, Carlos. I was sort of banking on the transition from one contract to another being seamless," she said. "I wasn't counting on much downtime, especially after having the time off at Christmas. But it looks like it may be a while before Chandler makes up his mind."

Saying the words aloud made her gut clench. All the uncertainty and fear she'd tamped down since Chandler announced he was temporarily putting the project on hold surged to the forefront.

He nodded. "That's what I want to talk to you about."

But then the elevator stopped and they had to dodge a gaggle of tourists as they stepped outside into the chill night. The cold January air was like a reality slap. Despite how Carlos put his arm around her as they walked, she had a bad feeling about what he'd come to say. A sense of foreboding hung in the air like an invisible fog, but when she glanced up, all that loomed above them was the Eiffel Tower, a giant decked out in lacy black steel silhouetted against the inky midnight sky.

They walked across the Champ de Mars lawn in the direction of the hotel, and for a long time neither of them said anything. She was determined to let him be the first to speak. Because in the meantime, they could simply walk arm in arm, through the lamp-lit streets of Paris and everything would be fine.

"I don't know how else to say this, Lindsay, other than to…just say it." His voice was thick with emotion. "I can't do this anymore."

There it was. The clock striking midnight, her coach morphing back into a pumpkin.

"Do what anymore? This?" She gestured back and forth between the two of them. "Do you mean *us?* Or—"

Her breath caught in her throat as if stopping her words. Good thing, too, because she hated the sarcasm in her voice, and the way her heart hammered at such a furious rate as if it were nailing her windpipe shut so that another word couldn't escape. Her hand fluttered to her neck. He reached out and grabbed her hand, lacing his fingers through hers.

"This has nothing to do with *us.*" The way he looked at her, his eyes so dark and full of raw sorrow, made her want to lean into him and wrap her arms around him. That, in turn, made her want to run. But she couldn't because of the firm grip he had on her hand.

"I realized today, I can't live my life in the public eye anymore. I'm just not cut out for it. And because of that, I would be holding you back."

"That's not true." Her voice was a hoarse whisper. "The show is going great. How can you just walk away from it now?"

With eyes full of torment, he searched her face, then ran a finger along her jawline. Her body responded to his touch and she hated herself for it. For God's sake, he was breaking up with her. How could she be so weak? But then again, weakness was what got her into this mess in the first place.

"You'll be fine. Chandler found you first. He'll simply revert back to the single-host *Diva Dishes* format, or there's no reason you can't drive the show yourself. Your talent is not dependent on me."

I'll be fine?

"So, if you're not re-signing for the show, what are you going to do?" she asked.

"I'm going back to Cedar Inlet and opening my restaurant."

It sounded like he had his mind made up.

"Great," she said. "I'll be on the road and you'll be in Florida. That doesn't sound very conducive to a relationship."

"It's the only way both of us will be happy, Lindsay."

She started backing up, trying to get away from him.

"So being apart will make you happy? That's certainly not the effect it'll have on me."

He shook his head. "I don't know what else to do," he said. "I can't stay, and I won't ask you to leave. It's killing me to do this, but I can't expect you to give up the show and follow me back to Cedar Inlet, to a restaurant that's still only the germ of an idea."

Through the tangle of emotions, she remembered what he'd said that night at dinner in Carcassonne; that he'd accepted the initial contract fully intending to take the money and run after he'd fulfilled his contractual obligation. She was the idiot for not seeing this coming—for blurring the lines between her professional and personal lives.

Fooled once, shame on the other guy; fooled twice…

Well, she was the fool.

"Just stop." She jerked her hand from his and took a big step back. When she did, her foot wobbled and she felt the slight drop of stepping onto an unsteady surface. But she righted herself without accepting his outstretched hand.

She glanced down and saw her right foot was on a sewer grate.

"You don't have to give me a sad, sad song and dance, Carlos." As she talked, she tried, as inconspicuously as possible, to free her heel from the grid. "All you have to say is, 'It's been fun, but I'm done here.' You're taking the money and running like you told me you were going to do."

"No, that's not—"

"Just stop! I don't want your reasons and excuses."

She wiggled her foot some more. To no avail. The damn thing was stuck.

Oh, God.

Why?

Why this? Why now?

She was such an idiot.

Tears welled in her eyes. All she wanted to do was leave. To get as far away from him as possible. "You don't have to pretend like it was anything more than it was—" She choked on her words.

As the first tear crested and fell, she curled her toes in her shoes and pulled with her right leg as hard as she could. The force sent her stumbling backward, but she was finally free.

Only when she started to run did she realize she'd broken the heel of her shoe.

Jimmy Choos be damned, there was no way she was going to turn around and get down on her hands and knees to pry the heel of her shoe out of a sewer grate. She'd suffered enough humiliation.

She just kept running.

Because there was no looking back now.

Chapter Fifteen

A week later, Lindsay sat at the kitchen table in her house in Trevard, North Carolina, talking to Ida May Higgins and spooning out chocolate chip cookie dough onto a baking sheet.

"It's nearly noon," said Ida May. "You know what you need, darlin'? You need to get yourself upstairs and take a good long shower, fix your hair and put on some color. Nothin' like a little color to perk up the mood."

She couldn't shower now. They were doing a taste test. Her mom's original recipe versus a variation that a well-known baking guru claimed was the best recipe *ever*. Ida had insisted on the taste test—immediately—despite how Lindsay suggested they do it another day. The last thing she needed was more sweets. She'd been trying to bake away her heartache since she'd been home, but it wasn't working.

First, she thought the brioche would do the trick, but that only reminded her of being with Carlos at the Leblanc Inn. She'd skipped her mom's Ultimate Cookie recipe because it would always and forever remind her of how he'd surprised her at Pâtisserie Delanoë. Instead, she made her mom's red velvet cake, three different kinds of pies and a double batch of coconut macaroons.

None of it worked.

"Of course not," Ida May had insisted. "Everyone knows *chocolate* is the cure for a broken heart, honey. You need chocolate chip cookies and you need them *now.* Because what's better for a broken heart than warm cookies with all that gooey, melty chocolate?"

As Ida May scraped dough from the sides of the bowl, she slanted a sidelong glance at Lindsay. "Have you heard anything from him, darlin'?"

Lindsay shook her head and tried to push the thought of Carlos from her mind. All week he'd been trying *not* to think of him.

She didn't blame him for not wanting to continue with the show. She wasn't even sure it was what she wanted anymore.

There was no job security in television. That had never been so clear as it was now, with Chandler holding up the show—and her life—while he tried to decide whether he wanted to take *The Diva Drives* to a full season.

He was hashing it out with sponsors, trying to *work out a deal.* Lindsay suspected he was buying time to see if he really wanted to move forward with her as the sole host of *Diva Drives,* or *Diva Dishes,* or...*ha ha Diva Dashes.*

Max told her Chandler hadn't been thrilled when she'd left Paris in the middle of the night—without saying goodbye. She'd called to apologize, but it had been a week and he'd yet to return her call.

It didn't bode well.

Sure, he was a busy man, but he was also very prone to changing his mind, especially if a venture didn't seem to be profitable.

Even more, common sense dictated that even if the *Diva* went to a full season, there would come a time when Carson Chandler turned his sights to newer, fresher…programming.

She supposed if her heart were really in the job, she'd fight for what she wanted, but Chandler's hemming and hawing over the show—keeping her future in limbo—reminded her that she really didn't *love* the television business, and how she hated putting her fate in someone else's hands. It had bothered her before when she'd reported for WKMO. But the *Diva* spot was a different format than dry news reporting. She'd thought it was a chance to be creative.

But really, the heart of the matter was that she wasn't in love with the job itself.

What she'd loved about it was working with Carlos. Spending time with him, getting to know him.

Falling in love with him.

She had enough money to tide her over for the time being, but she needed to have "Plan B" in the works so that she could invest her money rather than burn through it.

She sighed and looked up into the sweet, dark, wrinkled face of the woman who'd been the closest thing to a mother Lindsay had ever known. Ida May had helped her pick out prom dresses and held Lindsay's hand as she picked out the casket in which she buried her father.

When she'd gone over for Sophie's wedding Ida May had gladly watched the house. Then she extended the house-sitting for six weeks, insisting Lindsay accept Chandler's job offer.

And it was Ida May's shoulder she cried on for the first two days that she was back. She'd cried over Carlos; over the uncertainty of the show's future; over her future's murky forecast.

"That was a heavy sigh, darlin'," Ida May said as she reclaimed her chair at the table. "What are ya thinking?"

"That I missed you while I was gone."

The old woman reached out and took Lindsay's hand in hers. "I missed you, too, honey. But I can tell from looking at you that's not all that's on your mind."

Ida May knew her so well. It was comforting, but it also meant there was no place to hide when they were together.

"I'm twenty-nine years old, and I just can't seem to get it right."

The woman narrowed her eyes at Lindsay and cocked her head.

"I guess what I'm trying to say is if I have one regret in my life it's how I disappointed my father. I couldn't get my life together when he was alive. And I still haven't."

Ida May frowned and pulled herself up straight, a posture Lindsay knew meant the older woman was getting ready to speak, and she'd better listen.

"I have no idea what nonsense you're spouting. Aside from your mama, you were the love of your daddy's life. How is it you think you disappointed him?"

Lindsay closed her eyes for a moment, fighting off a sudden swell of tears, unexpected because she thought she'd cried herself dry earlier this week. But there was no mistaking the burning sensation stinging the backs of her lids.

Still, she took a deep breath and opened her eyes. "He always had such high hopes for me, and I let him down. I never lived up to his expectations. The only time I came halfway close was when I had the job with WKMO. I know it's crazy, he's been gone for four years now, but taking this job somehow felt like I was finally making good on all those years I let him down. But I couldn't sustain it."

God. She sounded pathetic. If there was one thing she hated it was playing the victim—a woman incapable of taking care of herself. She was just about to retract her pitiful dumping when Ida May said, "I assure you, your father was very proud of you. Lord, child, his only concern was that his daughter grew up to be a strong, independent woman. Someone who could take care of herself. I assure you if he could sit here at this table with us today, he'd be mighty proud of the woman you've become. The only way you could disappoint him is if you let yourself down."

There was a long stretch where neither of them said anything. Lindsay mulled over Ida's words.

Enough of this maudlin self-pity. It was time to put on her big-girl pants and figure out what was next—whether she should call Chandler again or have Max call Chandler to work his agenting magic. It seemed like what she *should* do. It was an opportunity that most people would die for.

But the thought of being away from home for months on end made her heart heavy. She didn't realize what a homebody she was until this week—being home, cooking in her own kitchen, sleeping in her own bed, sitting at her own table, talking to Ida May.

"Honey, if I can be honest with you, I think the only reason your daddy disliked you working as a receptionist was that he knew you weren't truly happy. Were you?"

Lindsay shook her head.

"What I think you need to do is search your soul and figure out your heart's desire. If it's being a television star then you need to get your butt on up to wherever Chandler is and demand that job—"

"That's the problem. I don't want it that bad. I really hated being away from home. This is where my heart is, and even if I don't quite know what the next step is, I'm fairly certain that's not it."

A smile spread across Ida May's face.

"You need to cross that one off the list. I think you need to give yourself a little credit for taking the leap of faith and trying it out. I hope you'll stay open-minded and take that leap again. 'Cause the only way you'll be a failure is if you close yourself off." She glanced at her watch again. "In the meantime, why don't you get yourself upstairs and fix yourself up like I suggested? I'll finish up here."

A shower would do her some good. She'd been lazy since she'd been home, sometimes staying in her pajamas until noon.

She put her arms around the old woman's beefy shoulders, breathing in the sweet scent of cookie dough, baby powder and sweat. "Ida May, have I told you how much I love you?"

The old woman squeezed Lindsay's hand. "Child, I love you, too. Now get yourself upstairs and tend to yours."

A dull, aching sadness settled in the pit of Lindsay's stomach. As she started toward the stairs, she counted her blessings, beginning with Ida May.

But before she could set foot on the first step, someone knocked on the front door.

"Oh, Lordy!" Ida May exclaimed from the kitchen. "I knew I should've hurried her up," the older woman murmured as she rushed into the living room.

When Lindsay turned to head back upstairs, Ida May said, "I suspect you'll want to get that."

Lindsay's hand was on the banister. "Well, I was just going to head back up—"

Ida May gave her head a quick shake. "No, ma'am. You'll definitely want to get this."

Puzzled, Lindsay studied the woman's wrinkled brown face as she walked toward the door. "What's going on, Ida May?"

Taking off her apron, the elder woman shrugged. "I reckon you ought to open the door and find out for yourself."

There was something in Ida May's eyes, which she quickly averted, that made Lindsay's heart quicken.

She opened the door and there was Carlos.

"Hello, I understand there's a woman here who lost a heel to a rather expensive pair of shoes. I've come to return it."

He pulled the heel to her Jimmy Choos out of his pocket and stood there holding it like a mini scepter.

"I would've been here sooner, but this thing was the devil to get loose from that storm drain. I hope you didn't throw the shoes out. I hope I'm not…too late? Am I?"

Lindsay threw her arms around him and held him as if she'd never let him go.

"Child, I tried to tell you to get yourself upstairs and get washed up," Ida May groused. "I told her to change clothes and put on some color. Never listens. Mmm-hmm. Never has from the time she was a tiny thing."

Lindsay turned and looked at Ida May. "You knew he was coming, didn't you?"

Ida May and Carlos smiled conspiratorially.

"Baby, you know how the story goes. Prince Charming always delivers the shoe. Well, in this case it was just the heel, but you'd have gotten no good out of those shoes without it."

Lindsay turned back to Carlos. "But how…? You two…?"

"I was afraid you wouldn't see me if I asked you if I could come," he said. "So, when I called the other day and got Ida May on the phone… Well, here I am. This time I don't intend to leave."

A sense of utter joy flooded through Lindsay. "But what about the restaurant?"

"I'm going to open it here."

Lindsay blinked. "Here in Trevard?"

He nodded. "I've spent the last week looking into business licenses and permits and facilities. Oh, and I heard there's a fabulous pastry chef in Trevard. She's sort of a diva, but I think the fact that she's self-taught fits right in with the concept of Out of the Fire. I've come to make her a partner. Do you think she'll accept?"

Epilogue

Four months later, Carlos and Lindsay opened the doors to Out of the Fire, a training restaurant for teens and young adults who'd gotten into trouble and needed a second chance.

A new direction.

A fresh start in life.

The rules for the on-the-job training program were rigid, but if a kid was willing to walk the straight-and-narrow and give one hundred-and-fifty percent, they just might qualify for one of twenty-five spots in the program.

Carlos fought off the nervous energy that was causing his heart to beat so furiously it was a wonder it didn't echo in the cavernous warehouse that they'd converted into a chic, ultramodern spot. Tonight was their first official test: prepare samples from the seasonal menu for the one hundred invited guests. Chandler, Max, Paula,

Sam and the whole *Diva* crew joined local dignitaries and regional food writers. Even Sophie, Luc and her daughter, Princess Savannah, flew in for the soft opening.

The Out of the Fire staff had worked nearly through the night prepping and planning so that the soft opening would wow the impressive guest list.

Carlos smoothed his moist palms on his black-and-white chef's pants as he watched a tall, slender boy who looked like he couldn't be more than sixteen or seventeen carry a tray full of Lindsay's desserts—everything from shortbread and chocolate chip cookies (her mother's recipe, of course), to fancy petits fours, cakes and tarts—toward the dessert tables.

The extensive work was paying off. The guests seemed to be enjoying themselves, and the night had all the signs of a successful soirée.

It was time for introductions of the kitchen staff and a champagne toast to christen their new venture. That meant Carlos faced just one more task. It was a pass or fail situation. He was sticking his neck out, taking a chance that quite frankly would either make him or break him.

He drew in a deep breath and pulled himself up to his full six-foot-four-inches, then gave Max the signal.

Max picked up a knife off an adjacent table and gently tapped it against his champagne flute.

"Could I have everyone's attention, please?"

The crowd quieted down in short order.

"Chef Carlos Montigo and I go way back. We've been through a lot together. That's why I'm honored to lift a glass in celebration tonight and toast the realization of my good friend's dream. This restaurant, the food you're eating tonight and the program that you all will find outlined in the brochures at your tables represents hard work, perseverance and frankly the investment of the chef's soul. However, even he didn't realize that in achieving all this—" Max gestured around the restaurant "—there would still be something missing. But I think he's figured out how to have it all. Before we introduce the kitchen staff, I'm going to turn the floor over to Carlos so he can tell you about that missing link. Chef?"

Hmm, this was a little different from what they'd discussed, Lindsay mused as she racked her brain for the missing link that Max spoke of. Maybe he'd found an investor for the program? It had to be something big to cause him to stray from the agenda.

Lost in thought she was suddenly aware that most every gaze in the room was riveted to her.

"Lindsay, would you join me over here?" Carlos repeated. "I promise I won't bite."

Waves of appreciative laughter rippled through the room.

Lindsay inclined her head to the side in a mock *I'm-not-so-sure* gesture.

As a partner in the restaurant, she wasn't surprised he wanted to introduce her. It's just that the evening's program was a bit out of order.

What did surprise her—in fact, it nearly knocked the wind out of her—was when Carlos took her hand and said, "I thought my dream would be realized when I finally opened the doors to Out of the Fire, but now that that has happened, I realized there is still a gaping hole right here."

He gestured to his heart. Then, as if in slow motion, Carlos reached into his pocket, pulled out a small black box, and knelt to the ground. "Even my life's work will not make me feel whole. The only way that will happen is if you will agree to be my wife."

Amidst the guests' gasps and sighs, Lindsay's head began to swim. For a moment all she could feel was the slow burning heat creeping up the back of her neck, making its way across her cheekbones. Carlos opened the box and held it out to her.

Her gaze was transfixed on the gorgeous diamond that seemed to light up the room.

"Will you do me the honor of being my wife?"

A slow scream of joy tried to bubble up her windpipe, but all she managed was a frantic nod and slightly guttural sound, which, at least, Carlos recognized as the yes she'd intended.

The crowd cheered as he slipped the ring on her finger.

Funny thing was, at that moment, the lyrics to "When You Wish upon a Star" drifted through her mind as if someone had turned on a radio. It was that part about the bolt from the blue pulling you through and how if you believe, your dreams really will come true. Well, she thought of that and how much she loved the man who was taking her into his arms.

In a moment, after the hysteria from the engagement celebration settled to a dull roar, Carson Chandler caught Lindsay's eye.

"I've just had a brilliant idea," he said. "How about a reality television show taped right here in your restaurant? Think about it...it'll be a natural winner..."

Lindsay smiled at him and turned back to her fiancé. This was all the reality she wanted. Right here in Carlos's arms.

* * * * *

Celebrate 60 years of pure reading pleasure with Harlequin®!

To commemorate the event, Silhouette Special Edition invites you to Ashley O'Ballivan's bed-and-breakfast in the small town of Stone Creek. The beautiful innkeeper will have her hands full caring for her old flame Jack McCall. He's on the run and recovering from a mysterious illness, but that won't stop him from trying to win Ashley back.

Enjoy an exclusive glimpse of Linda Lael Miller's
AT HOME IN STONE CREEK
Available in November 2009
from Silhouette Special Edition®

The helicopter swung abruptly sideways in a dizzying arch, setting Jack McCall's fever-ravaged brain spinning.

His friend's voice sounded tinny coming through the earphones. "You belong in a hospital," he said. "Not some backwater bed-and-breakfast."

All Jack really knew about the virus raging through his system was that it wasn't contagious, and there was no known treatment for it besides a lot of rest and quiet. "I don't like hospitals," he responded, hoping he sounded like his normal self. "They're full of sick people."

Vince Griffin chuckled, but it was a dry sound, rough at the edges. "What's in Stone Creek, Arizona?" he asked. "Besides a whole lot of nothin'?"

Ashley O'Ballivan was in Stone Creek, and she was a whole lot of somethin', but Jack had neither the strength nor the inclination to explain. After the way he'd ducked out six months before, he didn't expect a welcome, knew he didn't deserve one. But Ashley, being Ashley, would take him in whatever her misgivings.

He had to get to Ashley; he'd be all right.

He closed his eyes, letting the fever swallow him.

There was no telling how much time had passed when he became aware of the chopper blades slowing overhead. Dimly, he saw the private ambulance waiting on the airfield outside of Stone Creek; it seemed that twilight had descended.

Jack sighed with relief. His clothes felt clammy against his flesh. His teeth began to chatter as two figures unloaded a gurney from the back of the ambulance and waited for the blades to stop.

"Great," Vince remarked, unsnapping his seat belt. "Those two look like volunteers, not real EMTs."

The chopper bounced sickeningly on its runners, and Vince, with a shake of his head, pushed open his door and jumped to the ground, head down.

Jack waited, wondering if he'd be able to stand on his own. After fumbling unsuccessfully with the buckle on his seat belt, he decided not.

When it was safe the EMTs approached, following Vince, who opened Jack's door.

His old friend Tanner Quinn stepped around Vince, his grin not quite reaching his eyes.

"You look like hell warmed over," he told Jack cheerfully.

"Since when are you an EMT?" Jack retorted.

Tanner reached in, wedged a shoulder under Jack's right arm and hauled him out of the chopper. His knees immediately buckled, and Vince stepped up, supporting him on the other side.

"In a place like Stone Creek," Tanner replied, "everybody helps out."

They reached the wheeled gurney, and Jack found himself on his back.

Tanner and the second man strapped him down, a process that brought back a few bad memories.

"Is there even a hospital in this place?" Vince asked irritably from somewhere in the night.

"There's a pretty good clinic over in Indian Rock," Tanner answered easily, "and it isn't far to Flagstaff." He paused to help his buddy hoist Jack and the gurney into the back of the ambulance. "You're in good hands, Jack. My wife is the best veterinarian in the state."

Jack laughed raggedly at that.

Vince muttered a curse.

Tanner climbed into the back beside him, perched on some kind of fold-down seat. The other man shut the doors.

"You in any pain?" Tanner said as his partner climbed into the driver's seat and started the engine.

"No." Jack looked up at his oldest and closest friend and wished he'd listened to Vince. Ever since he'd come down with the virus—a week after snatching a five-year-old girl back from her noncustodial parent, a small-time Colombian drug dealer—he hadn't been able to think about anyone or anything but Ashley. When he *could* think, anyway.

Now, in one of the first clearheaded moments he'd experienced since checking himself out of Bethesda the day before, he realized he might be making a major mistake. Not by facing Ashley—he owed her that much and a lot more. No, he could be putting her in danger, putting Tanner and his daughter and his pregnant wife in danger, too.

"I shouldn't have come here," he said, keeping his voice low.

Tanner shook his head, his jaw clamped down hard as though he was irritated by Jack's statement.

"This is where you belong," Tanner insisted. "If you'd had sense enough to know that six months ago, old buddy, when you bailed on Ashley without so much as a fare-thee-well, you wouldn't be in this mess."

Ashley. The name had run through his mind a million times in those six months, but hearing somebody say it out loud was like having a fist close around his insides and squeeze hard.

Jack couldn't speak.

Tanner didn't press for further conversation.

The ambulance bumped over country roads, finally hitting smooth blacktop.

"Here we are," Tanner said. "Ashley's place."

* * * * *

Will Jack be able to patch things up with Ashley,
or will his past put the woman he loves in harm's way?
Find out in
AT HOME IN STONE CREEK
by Linda Lael Miller
Available November 2009
from Silhouette Special Edition®

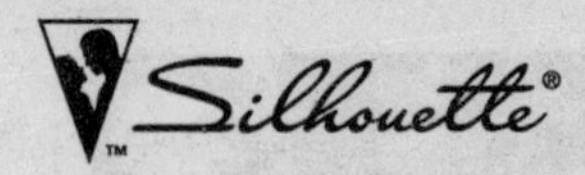

SPECIAL EDITION®

COMING NEXT MONTH

Available October 27, 2009

#2005 AT HOME IN STONE CREEK—Linda Lael Miller
Sometimes Ashley O'Ballivan felt like the only single woman left in Stone Creek. All because of security expert Jack McCall—the man who broke her heart years ago. Now Jack was mysteriously back in town…and Ashley's single days were numbered.

#2006 A LAWMAN FOR CHRISTMAS—Marie Ferrarella
Kate's Boys
When a car accident landed her mother in the hospital, it was Kelsey Marlowe's worst nightmare. Luckily, policeman Morgan Donnelly was there to save her mom, and the nightmare turned into a dream come true—as Kelsey fell hard for the sexy lawman!

#2007 QUINN McCLOUD'S CHRISTMAS BRIDE—Lois Faye Dyer
The McClouds of Montana
Wolf Creek's temporary sheriff Quinn McCloud was a wanderer; librarian Abigail Foster was the type to set down roots. But when they joined forces to help a little girl left on Abigail's doorstep, did opposites ever attract! And just in time for a Christmas wedding.

#2008 THE TEXAN'S DIAMOND BRIDE—Teresa Hill
The Foleys and the McCords
When Travis Foley caught gemologist Paige McCord snooping around on his property for the fabled Santa Magdalena Diamond, it spelled trouble for the feuding families. But what was it about this irresistible interloper that gave the rugged rancher pause?

#2009 MERRY CHRISTMAS, COWBOY!—Cindy Kirk
Meet Me in Montana
All academic Lauren Van Meveren wanted from her trip to Big Sky country was peace and quiet to write her dissertation. But when she moved onto widower Seth Anderssen's ranch to help with his daughter, Lauren got the greatest gift of all—true love.

#2010 MOONLIGHT AND MISTLETOE—Dawn Temple
When her estranged father sent Beverly Hills attorney Kyle Anderson to strong-arm her into a settlement, Shayna Miller was determined to resist…until Kyle melted her heart and had her heading for the nearest mistletoe, head-over-heels in love….

SSECNMBPA1009